Child Support

Child Support

Amour

www.urbanbooks.net

Urban Books, LLC
97 N 18th Street
Wyandanch, NY 11798

ISBN 13: 978-1-60162-638-7
ISBN 10: 1-60162-638-X

First Mass Market Printing December 2014
First Trade Paperback Printing October 2012
Printed in the United States of America

10 9 8 7 6 5 4 3 2 1

*This is a work of fiction. Any references or similar-
ities to actual events, real people, living or dead, or
to real locales are intended to give the novel a sense
of reality. Any similarity in other names, characters, places, and incidents is entirely coincidental.*

Distributed by Kensington Publishing Corp.
Submit Wholesale Orders to:
Kensington Publishing Corp.
C/O Penguin Group (USA) Inc.
Attention: Order Processing
405 Murray Hill Parkway
East Rutherford, NJ 07073-2316
Phone: 1-800-526-0275
Fax: 1-800-227-9604

Acknowledgments

AMOUR thanks: First and foremost, I want to thank the man upstairs for blessing me with the ability to write and also the opportunity to live out my dreams. Next, my mother, who did her best to give my sister and me the world, I can't thank you enough. My favorite sister in the whole wide world, Sanny Stax, I love you big money! My other two sisters, who I love dearly, Pebblez and Carlina. My granny, who is the backbone of our family, you're so giving and loving. You made being a teen mom so much easier for me with all the doctoring and help you gave. I love you, turkey. Jerry, I want to thank you also. You were my superman as a child. My nieces McKenzie and Mari.

My heartbeat and the reason behind everything I choose to do, my Sexyman. Mommy has no clue where she'd be without you. Love you, Li'l Redd. I want to thank the one who helped me make our bundle of joy, Big Redd. I probably wouldn't have written a book if you hadn't suggested it. This is more than a relationship; it's indescribable. I love you more than you'll ever know. My favorite cousins, Nikki and Dora, you guys were my support system, and I'm thankful for everything you have done for me. First, you gave me this brilliant idea and also helped me to make my dream come true. Thank you a million. Joy, thanks for repping me and keeping me posted on everything. The Urban Book family. My gals who keep my life entertaining, BG, Chrystal, Snook, Ariana, Niqua, Mariah, and my boo, Tia. My guy best friend, who is more like the brother I never had, LL Cool LA. I also want to thank my extended family, the Richardsons.

The city of Toledo, the home of my very first fans, no matter where I go, I will never forget where I came from. I want to give a very special thank-you to my fifth grade reading teacher, who thought the poem I wrote for an assignment was a song I had stolen off the radio and made me submit something else. I was hurt then, but now I realize how talented I was at the age of ten. My dad, although I may never understand your choices in life, I want to thank you. I probably wouldn't be where I am today had you had more time for us. I turned out great! Last but not least, I want to thank *you* who purchased this book. I promise you're going to enjoy it.

First thanks: To my Lord and Savior Jesus Christ, without you nothing is possible, and thank you for your favor! Jazmyn and Asia, I need and want big sister to look out for little sis, and I would never trade in the best daughters in the entire world, Daddy's little girls! Montre and Bryce, be better and work harder than me! You guys, always remember dreams come true as long as you believe, 'cause I believe in you guys. Daddy loves you! Thank you to Mother, Yvette Tonia. Thank you for teaching and showing me that hard work will always pay off. I love you, Mom! Thank you to Kimberly Mckenzie and Apryle Ayala for giving me great kids. Both of you are two of the best mothers a father can have.

To my FM team, Mark Moosh Courtney. You guys already know how I feel. Techa Lewis, my boss chick! Lisa Hawkins, Happy Birthday February 1, LOL. My 1stGen Publishing team, Ni'chelle Genovese, no matter what, I got you! Shad, aka The Game, Authir KA$H, Shareef, and Anjela. AMOUR, for helping me with this novel. Renee Jones, my reader-reviewer, my friend, thank you. Renee, tell your mother I said I love the Jones family! Joylynn, the super book agent! Charleen and Simone at Urban knowledge bookstore, thank you for supporting me every step of the way with this book game. Governor Washington G-Unit, we on tour, baby. Trina and Kaliah, thank you so much. Words can't express how I feel right now. I love you guys.

To my entire Facebook family, Shawnda, Anjela, Detra, Carolyn, Tara, Brooke. Shalanda you got milk. Gwen B, love ya, sis. My Nasty Ms. Nasty Cherly, I'm your brother. Lisa Jeter, thank you for being real. Theresa Bishop, my class of '91. Ray and Linda Boyce, Dottie, Curtis, Shaka, Jess, Toya, Larry Jr., Louis, Mildred, Tinisha, the Worlds family, Sharita T-black, my family no matter what happens. To my father, Thomas Hawkins, who never got the chance for the world to see his talent. If you're a Hawkins, Tonia, Brown, Riddick, Boyce, this is for us! Family first!

Chapter 1

As my phone danced on my cherrywood nightstand, I sat up in bed and looked over to see who was calling me. It was my mother. Every time she called, I was instantly annoyed. The bad part about it was she barely called me to begin with. I hesitated before answering.

"Yes, Mom?"

"Don't start with me, Angel. I just called to see if you took your medicine."

I rolled my eyes. I hated taking that medicine, and she knew it. What I hated most was her treating me as if I were a child.

"Yes, I took it," I answered, knowing I was lying.

She hung up right after that.

My mother and I had drifted apart many years ago due to her feeling as though I had ruined her life. I didn't exactly know how I could have done that, but from the time I hit fifteen to the time I moved out of her house, she reminded me daily.

I hadn't taken my pills, so I decided to get up and do so. I went downstairs to get some ice water, and then I headed upstairs to my bathroom. I opened the cabinet and pulled out the two bottles of pills. I stared at them for a moment. I decided that I was going to take only one prescription, popping one of the bottles open.

I read, "Lithium is for manic depression. Use as prescribed by physician," as I did every time I decided to take my meds. I took the directed number of pills, guzzling them down.

My phone made a loud buzzing noise on my nightstand. I walked out of my bathroom and went to get it. I picked it up and saw that it was Pat.

I had met Pat at my daytime job. I was a secretary at a prestigious law firm in Chicago. After he'd done a lot of begging and pleading, I decided to go out with him.

"Miss Jacobs, why don't you l-l-let a nigga take y-y-you out tonight?" he'd asked.

I'd screwed my face up and replied, "No thanks." I tried my best to be polite and not tell him what I really thought, which was he was too damn big and I could not stand all that stuttering.

"Why n-n-not? Y-y-you'll love it. I pr-pr-promise to treat you right," he'd replied, trying to convince me.

I shook my head.

He just would not take no for an answer. He was leaning his heavyset body on the counter above my desk.

I stared at my computer screen and continued setting appointments, which was what I was doing before he approached me. I decided that I wouldn't respond to his repetitive questions.

"Ex-ex-excuse me," he said while patting the counter loudly.

"What?" I gave him my attention. I didn't want my boss, Mr. Bennifeld, to hear any of this.

"What's up?" he asked.

"Okay, I'll go," I said, giving in. I wrote my number down for him, and then he left, satisfied. In disgust, I watched him walk out the door.

A whole hour hadn't passed, and he was already calling my phone. I was annoyed when I answered and heard his voice on the line. He said we were going out to eat, and that was it. I was absolutely sure that was all we would do, because he wasn't cute enough to do anything else with . . . at least not with me.

I told him I was about to jump in the shower and that I would call him once I was finished. As soon as I hung up with him, I went into the bathroom to do as I'd said. After twenty minutes had passed, I stepped out of the shower and found myself standing in front of my full-body mirror, admiring my dripping wet body. I stared at my small frame. My flawless face and deep dimples simply made me a beauty. I touched my hair, which I had just gotten done. There was something about my healthy black hair that kept me feeling stunning. Although my shoulder-length hair had lost a few curls from the steam of the shower, it still looked good.

I grabbed my towel off the toilet seat and began to dry off. After I was completely dry, I lathered lotion all over my body, thinking of what I could possibly wear. I didn't want to appear too sexy, because I didn't want to tease him too much. I decided to wear a pair of blue jeans, neutral-colored heels, and a hunter-green vest. It was plain, but it would do. I wasn't really the flashy type, anyway. I thought being a plain Jane was a good thing.

I heard my BlackBerry going off in my room, so I ran to get it. As expected, it was Pat.

"Yes?" I said with irritation. He had called me all of twenty minutes ago.

"You 'b-b-bout ready?" he stuttered.

I told him that I needed at least fifteen more minutes.

He said, "Okay." And then we hung up.

"So damn annoying," I said aloud. I went to my closet to get the items that I had mentally put together, and then I began to put them on. I searched my jewelry drawer for the appropriate gold accessories to put on. After I accomplished that, I retrieved my tan handbag and sprayed on my body mist. Then my phone began to ring, again.

I already knew it was Pat, so I just picked up. "I'm coming out the door," I said and hung up. I knew at that moment that this would be our first and last date.

I entered my little sister's room to check on her. She wasn't in there. I had totally forgotten that I had sent her off with my childhood best friend, Tiffany. I figured it was my meds that had made me forget; temporary memory loss was one of the side effects.

I shut her bedroom door and headed down the steps.

Pat was all smiles when I slid inside of his car. His 350-pound frame was overpowering his seat. His missing tooth almost made me throw up in my own mouth. He resembled a beat-down Bruce Bruce, but with none of the style that Bruce had. I turned my head and looked out the window on my side of the car.

He put his hand on my thigh and rubbed it. I shot him an evil look, and he quickly removed it. *This fool has lost his mind.* We pulled off and headed to our destination. The car ride was pretty silent at first, until Pat decided to speak.

"So you gl-gl-glad you decided to come ch-ch-chill with a nigga?"

I turned to look at him and smiled. In my head I said, *Hell no,* but out of my mouth I said, "Yeah. So far, so good."

"Yeah, I'm happy y-y-you came too. I'm gon' t-t-take you to a five-st-star restaurant since you a five-st-st-star bitch," he said with a smile.

I didn't know why he felt that that statement was okay to say. I didn't care what word you put before *bitch;* in my world it was still inappropriate.

"Please don't call me out my name," I said politely. I turned my attention back to the scene out my window.

"Wh-wh-why you tripping?"

Is he serious? This man was working my nerves already. I turned back to him.

"Tripping?"

"Yeah," he answered.

I guess he really felt I had no reason to be upset. "Why can't you respect the fact I don't like being called any kind of bitch?" I asked.

He just shook his head and focused on the road. I could tell this date would be sour, and I was impatiently waiting for it to be over.

We ended up at Keefer's, a five-star steak house. As I stepped out of the car, I hoped and prayed that I wouldn't see anyone I knew. Outside the car, Pat was a huge disaster. His beard needed a trimming, and he needed his hair braided. His outfit and shoes were the only things that let one know he had some kind of money. Too bad money couldn't make up for his weight, looks, or that nasty-ass attitude.

"Y-y-you first, my l-l-lady," he said as he held the door open.

I silently chuckled as I walked into the restaurant. He was trying to get back on good terms with me. The Keefer's staff looked at us in astonishment. I knew they were wondering how he had pulled this one off . . . with me, that is.

"Table for two?" the host asked us.

Pat shook his head yes as a young, perky Hispanic girl grabbed two menus and told us to follow her. She stopped in front of a table that had a chair on each side. She set the menus down in front of us and told us the day's special as we took our seats. We told her what we were drinking, and she was on her way.

"Angel, why you acting l-l-like you ain't feeling a n-n-nigga?" Pat decided to ask.

You think, I thought.

"Pat, why you bugging? Can we just enjoy this date, or what?" I responded. It was a good thing that he knew I wasn't interested in him, though. I thought maybe he'd just give up after trying over and over again and never getting anywhere with me.

"I—I—I mean, yeah, but you on th-th-that fake sh-sh-shit," he answered.

I told him, "If I didn't like you, Pat, you would know."

As he continued to run his stuttering mouth, I noticed something far more interesting. He made his way into the restaurant and sat two tables behind ours. He was wearing an expensive black suit and reading the *Chicago Tribune.* In my eyes, that said "Money" loud enough for me to hear.

I watched his every move and didn't pay Pat any kind of attention. When the server came back to take our order, I could hardly order, because I was focused on Mr. Expensive in the back. I wanted so badly to go fuck the lights out of him.

"Angel!" Pat yelled while hitting the table to get my attention.

I snapped out of my trance. "What? Damn!"

"If yo' sl-sl-slut ass wasn't all in th-th-that nigga face, you would've heard m-m-me say we 'bout to order," he stuttered.

We placed our orders, and the waitress went on her way. I continued to gaze at Mr. Expensive, but I tried to be discreet about it. We sat there in total silence until the waitress brought us our meals.

When we finished, I said, "Well, Pat, we're going to need to bring this little date to an end soon. I have to be at work in an hour."

"All . . . all . . . all right. Let me g-g-get you some desser-ser-sert first," he insisted.

He flagged the waitress down, and she sa-shayed over to our table. I guess he was asking me what I wanted, but I was too caught up in Mr. Expensive chewing his steak so perfectly that I didn't hear a word he said. He started pounding on the table again. I snapped out of my trance and gave him an evil look. I almost started to curse his big ass out, but I decided to let him pass this time.

When the server brought out our bill for the drinks and meals, Pat paid for them, and we left. During the walk to the car, I wondered if running back into the restaurant to give Mr. Expensive my number would be rude. I changed my mind after I looked at how mad Pat was. He struggled getting in his way too small Lincoln MKZ.

"Y-y-you one disrespectful-ass b-b-bitch," he spat as soon as he managed to get in.

"Excuse me," was all I could say.

"Ex-ex-excuse you? No, bitch, excuse me," he yelled as he drove away from the restaurant. He had called me one too many bitches, and that was where I drew the line. I started cursing back at him. After a lot of screaming and too much miscommunication, he stopped the car.

"Bitch, get out," he said loud and clear.

I twisted my face up. There was no way in hell I was getting out and walking anywhere. I sat there. He threw his door open and climbed out of the car. He speedily came over to my side of the car. I had no time to think of locking the doors. He opened my door and tightly grabbed my arm. I was sure he left a mark.

"Get yo' muthafucking hands off of me!" I yelled.

He yanked me out of the car and lifted me in the air. He then placed me on the ground. After I landed on my ass, he headed back to the driver's side of his car. Cars slowly rolled past as they watched him embarrass the hell out of me.

I jumped up. "You stuttering bitch," I yelled at him. I was pissed and humiliated.

"Fuck you," he yelled back. He got in his car faster than he got out and sped off.

I looked down at my grass-stained jeans. My vest and the back of my pants were muddy. It had rained the day before, and unfortunately, the grass was still very wet. A tear fell from my eyes as I picked my purse up from the ground. I opened it and retrieved my phone. It read 8:55 p.m. I had to hurry and get home. I had to be at my night job no later than 9:50. I had to make this forty-five-minute walk a thirty-minute one.

It wasn't that I needed two jobs. I just enjoyed the money. I loved being independent and getting the things that I wanted. I rarely worked at my second job. In fact, I probably worked two weekends out of the month there, if that.

I began my long journey home with my head held low. I was beyond annoyed at the hooting and the hollering by the thirsty men that drove past, not to mention the eye-problem-having females that stared and glared as they sped past too. Already I could tell that this was going to be a long night.

A horn beeped behind me, so I cautiously turned around to see what car it had come from. It was a smoky-gray Bentley with tinted windows. I became skeptical as it pulled over to the side of the road. I was almost certain that it wasn't a serial killer or a rapist, being that they were riding in a 150,000-dollar car.

The car lights shone in my eyes. I covered the glare with my hand. Reluctantly, I walked to the car. As much as I didn't want to get in the car, I really didn't want to walk all the way home. When I got to the driver's side window, I wondered who could be sitting on the other side of it. The window rolled down slowly. The smell of Black Ice car freshener escaped the car. To my surprise, it was Mr. Expensive pushing this whip. Something told me that the brother was paid . . . but *damn!*

"Now, I know I just seen you with a guy. What happened?"

I stood there wondering if I should tell him the truth or make up something. What I did know was that he was very attractive, and I was glad that he was the driver of this whip.

"Well, my date saw how I was looking at you, and he got all upset," I said in all honesty. Mr. Expensive smiled, revealing his perfect pearly whites.

"I can't understand how a beautiful lady like you would be walking all alone. If you don't mind, I'd like to give you a ride home."

I didn't hesitate as I walked over to the passenger side to hop in. Once I was in, I started checking the luxurious car out. I had never been in anything with so much worth as this, and I was feeling like royalty.

I gave him the directions to where I lived, and then we were off. When we pulled up to my two-story home, I thanked him.

"Before you go, would it be asking too much for a name and maybe a number?" he asked.

I smiled and said, "No, it wouldn't. My name is Angel," and then I gave him my number.

He quickly typed my name and number into his iPhone. "I'm Mitch. . . . I want to see you again, sooner than later," he proclaimed.

"Well, you can see me tonight. That's if you don't mind coming to a nightclub," I said, believing he would decline. I assumed a nightclub in Chicago would be too much for him.

"Cool. Which one? You ain't no stripper, are you?" he asked.

"No, I'm a bartender at Vision Nightclub. Come. I'll hook you up with the drinks." I ended our conversation there as I stepped out of his car. I was hoping he would come, but I didn't want to get my hopes up too high. I waved to him as I opened my front door.

He blew the horn, and then he pulled off.

Normally, I didn't get swept off my feet that easily, but Mitch was another breed. At this point,

I was somewhat glad that Pat had yanked me out of his car. I knew I had to be extra sexy tonight, especially if Mitch was going to be present.

I stood behind the bar making the drinks, which people consistently ordered. I always studied the many different people who ordered drinks or worked the dance floor. Everyone had a story, and some people's facial expressions told it all.

A muscular, chocolate-coated man slid in the seat that was directly in front of me. He was looking down at something, but in my mind, I knew he had money on top of money, because his Armani suit said that he did.

"What you drinking?" I asked as I leaned over the counter so that he could hear my voice over the loud music. I wanted him to look up so that I could see his face.

"Two shots of Hennessy and bottled water," he replied. I was shocked he was drinking dark liquor. He looked to me like a Cîroc or Goose drinker, but I went to work, anyway, as I got his shot glass and the Hennessy off the shelf. I poured the cups and slid them to him. Then I went to the cooler and retrieved his bottled water.

"Twelve," I said as I sat the water on the counter. He pulled out a Gucci wallet and took a twenty-dollar bill out. He handed it to me.

"Keep the change."

I smiled. As long as I had been working there, no one had ever tipped me over two dollars. I wasn't fazed by the eight dollars. *He* fazed me. He defined the term *sexy*, and I could tell that wifey was not doing her job, obviously. As he looked up and smiled, I couldn't help but smile back at him. It was Mitch, and I knew God was giving me a sign.

I could feel my juices sliding down my inner thighs. I was hoping they wouldn't go through my tight blue jean shorts. I wanted more, so I decided to spark up a conversation.

"You seem out of your element," I said, leaning in so he could hear me. His eyes zoomed in on my breasts. After all, they were poking out of my low-cut shirt.

He finally found my eyes. "Yeah, just a little, but I'll be fine." He cracked a small smile.

He left the bar shortly after our conversation. The remainder of the night, my eyes searched the room for him every so often, but I didn't see him.

"Girl, he got you open," said my drunken coworker Brittany. She laughed.

I turned toward her with a smile on my face, handing her another Sex on the Beach. I shook my head no, because I wasn't open at all. I just had my mind set on him.

When the night ended, I gathered my things and headed out the door. To my surprise, there was Mitch, leaning up against his Bentley. He was parked in front of the club, and I couldn't help but blush, knowing that he was waiting on me.

"Thought I left without you, huh?" He smiled.

I shook my head no, knowing damn well I was lying. "Follow me," I said as I seductively walked to my car, three cars behind. I could feel his eyes on me, and I liked every minute of it.

After we pulled up to my two-story house, I parked and hopped out of the car. He followed suit, trailing me to my door. When we got inside, I turned on the living room lamp and the TV. We both sat on the plush love seat. There was a lull in the conversation, so I decided to revive it.

"Any kids?" I questioned.

"No, ma'am. You?"

"Well, I have a daughter, but her dad is keeping her from me."

"Really? Why, if you don't mind me asking?" he asked.

Even though I hated talking about it, I figured it would not hurt to tell him. "Well, he and his family thought I was crazy, and were upset that I didn't want to be with him anymore," I said, telling half the truth.

"Wow," was all Mitch could say.

Truthfully, I was a little crazy, according to the doctor who had diagnosed me with bipolar disorder years ago. Sometimes, I did question my sanity when I did things I wouldn't normally do, but I couldn't control myself in some situations. It wasn't my fault . . . or maybe it was since I refused to take the medicine that was prescribed me. I hadn't done anything abnormal in over a month, so I didn't feel the need to take the pills all the time. They only made me feel drowsy, and I didn't have time for that.

I decided to invite him up to my room. My sister was gone, and it was very seldom that I had the house to myself. As soon as I closed the bedroom door behind us, Mitch and I started kissing. I pushed him down onto the bed. I sat down next to him. He sat up, removing my clothes from my body, and I returned the favor.

I climbed on top of him once we were totally naked. I popped my pussy on his big black dick. I already knew tonight would be a night that he would never forget. He held my body close to his as I continued riding him like at a rodeo. My hands slid under the pillows to grip the sheets.

My left hand felt something that I thought I had got rid of a month ago. Mitch began whispering in my ear.

"Show Daddy what you got."

I sped up my pace, and then I instantly got pissed. I looked him in his face and saw my baby daddy. I just started stabbing him recklessly with the machete I had under the pillow. He screamed like a little bitch, but I couldn't stop laughing as I continued to ride his dick.

"You like that, Daddy?" I asked in a seductive tone while licking my lips.

He just grunted, as all the men did. His blood splashed on me and all over the walls. He still wasn't dead, though. For some odd reason it appeared he had nine lives.

I grabbed his hand and rubbed it across my clit. His hand was a little cold. I placed his hand on my thigh and turned his arm so that the inside of his wrist was visible to me. His vein poked out, begging me to make it leak. I could hear it screaming, "Angel, slice me." Therefore, I did.

His eyes rolled in the back of his head, and his body shut down. I wasn't sure if he had gone to meet his maker or if he was playing possum. His blood was dripping out of his wrist and onto my thigh.

"Uh-oh, baby, we're making a big mess," I said as I wiped the blood off with his hand. I continued to ride him, thrusting my body up and down on his dick. I wasn't sure if he came or not. I mean, I didn't want him to get blue balls.

Something kept telling me that he was still alive, and I just couldn't have that. I mean, after all the evil shit he had done, he didn't deserve to live. I started my stabbing spree back up. I let the machete land wherever it wanted to. Even though my arm was tired, I continued to stab him.

I heard knocks on the door shortly after. I hurriedly hopped off his dick and ran to the door. I cracked the door and peeked through the opening. There was no one there. Maybe I was tripping. I closed the door and locked it behind me. I walked back over to the bed and saw that he had blood coming from his mouth.

I smiled a devious smile. I stood over him, shaking my head. His six-foot, solid, chocolate frame lay there lifelessly. I grabbed my machete, which had obviously fallen onto the floor when I went to answer the door.

"Well, since you're dead, you won't be needing this," I said as I grabbed his dick. I pressed my machete up against it and slowly cut it off. It gave me a natural high to know he wouldn't be fucking any other bitch, let alone getting one pregnant.

I put on my silk robe and headed outside to the backyard with his dick in my hand. My pit bull, Concrete, loved meat. I was sure that this was some meat she had never had. I opened up her gate and placed it in her dog bowl. When I stepped out of the way, she immediately began chowing down on it. I closed the gate and watched her for a while, and then I headed back inside. I had a mess to clean and a man to get rid of.

First, I went straight to the bathroom to wash my hands. The sink was full of blood mixed with water. The color turned me on. I damn near had an orgasm watching it flow down the drain.

When my hands were clean, I decided to head upstairs to get that bum out of my house. He was a deadbeat-ass father, and I hated him. All these years of keeping me from our daughter and he really thought he was going to get in my pants and not suffer the consequences? A fool he was.

I opened my bedroom door, and there was blood all over the place. This was definitely going to be a task. I went to retrieve my first-aid kit and sewing box out of my closet. I grabbed the chair from my vanity and placed it next to the bed. I sat down on it and grabbed his arm with the wrist that I had sliced and began stitching him back up. I figured that if I stitched him, he wouldn't bleed so much when I put his clothes back on.

After that was completed, I got a bucket and filled it with some hot water, grabbed a couple of washcloths, and gave him a bed bath. Surprisingly, I hadn't stabbed his face. He still looked presentable from the neck up. That was exactly how I needed him to be so when people saw him in his car, they would assume he had fallen asleep at the wheel and he wasn't sitting there dead.

After I washed him good, I wrapped his arms up with bandages. They both were sliced and diced from the stabbing spree I went on. I put the clothes he'd been wearing back on him. Good thing he'd worn a suit, because he definitely needed long sleeves. When he was completely dressed, I dragged him out of the bed and to the hallway by the stairs. He was already dead, so there was no need to be gentle with him. I rolled his ass down the stairs. His head hit all thirteen stairs hard.

I laughed the entire time. I was starting to feel bad for him, but not bad enough to forgive him for what he had done. When he reached the bottom, I walked down the stairs and retrieved my red leather gloves off of the coffee table. I put them on and got his keys out of his suit jacket.

I clicked the automatic unlock button to his smoky-gray Bentley as I dragged him out to his car. I opened the passenger door and struggled putting him in the seat. It took me about a half an hour of struggling before I got him settled in. I decided I wouldn't put his seat belt on. I mean, how much more dead could he get? Then I got behind the wheel and started the ignition. The clock read 4:54 a.m. I knew I had to rush, because soon it would be daylight. I parked his car two blocks from my house and placed him in the driver's seat. I looked around and didn't see a soul in sight. I decided to leave the car running, and then I jogged back home.

I was out of breath by the time I made it back home. Handling his body and jogging home were a bit much for me. I was tired, so I went upstairs to my room to clean up the mess I had made and get some sleep.

I woke up at 8:00 a.m., as I did every morning for work. After a refreshing shower, I went to wake up my little sister, Crystal, for school. I opened her bedroom door to find that she was not in the bed.

"Right. She's over at Tiffany's," I said to myself out loud. I closed her door and headed down the stairs to find something quick to eat.

Crystal had been living with me ever since our mother had been diagnosed with cancer. Crystal had Down syndrome and anxiety attacks. I was about fifteen years older than her. When we were growing up, it always seemed as though my mother didn't care for her, but because she was her daughter, she had to stand her. I never understood or questioned it, though, but I figured it was because she had all those health problems.

I would have loved it if Crystal were my daughter, being that I lost my child in a tragic situation. I was fifteen when I got pregnant. I didn't quite remember who I had sex with when I got pregnant with her, because I was pissy drunk that night. When I had her, I was in a psych ward for suicidal attempts. She and Crystal would have been the same age, eight years old.

I sat at the table as I ate my breakfast and listened to the news. The reporter mentioned a death in Lincoln Park, which was my neighborhood. I grabbed the remote and turned up the TV.

"We have breaking news. There has been another death here in Chicago. The body was found in a gray Bentley over in the Lincoln Park area. This is the third death of a male in the last two weeks. We are not sure if the deaths are connected as of yet, but this is very coincidental," the blond-haired, blue-eyed reporter announced. "The body belonged to thirty-four-year-old Mitchell Perry." They posted a recent picture of him on the screen so that everyone could see exactly what he looked like when he was alive. "If you know anything about this case, please call the police station at five-five-five-two-three-four-one, or Crime Stoppers at five-five-five-oh-eight-one-two."

I felt bad, and my stomach started to hurt. I got up and went to the bathroom. I lifted the toilet seat and vomited. I wiped my mouth off with a washcloth and headed back to the kitchen. That was too close for comfort. That was right around the corner from our house, and we lived in a good neighborhood. The thought of a murder so close to home was a bit much for me.

I had lost my appetite, so I dumped the rest of my breakfast in the trash, headed upstairs to brush my teeth, then came back downstairs and walked out the door. I climbed in my car; then I headed to the law firm. I worked at Bennifeld's law firm in Chicago, a place many, many criminals called home. I met at least five new people a day.

The majority of people who entered the law firm were males who had caught a case and knew this was the best place to receive help. They had to talk money, because Mr. Bennifeld was very expensive. This was where I met some of my male friends, but I met the majority at my bartending night job at Vision Nightclub.

I parked my Ford Taurus in my assigned parking spot and turned my car off. I sat in my car a few minutes before stepping out. I was still feeling a bit sick, not to mention that I felt a little cold coming on. I hugged myself, trying to get warm. It was late September, and it was beginning to get chilly outside.

My red BeBe heels clinked against the pavement as I made my way inside of the firm. When I was growing up, people labeled me a stuck-up, skinny chick, but in my eyes I was just selective about who I conversed with. Without a doubt, I was pretty, but I wasn't conceited. I was just aware of my beauty. All my clothes weren't name brands, but they were all well put together. My flawless cocoa-brown skin complimented my light brown eyes and my five-five frame.

At the law office I was this uppity, proper lady. At night at the club I was a very different person. I think this was very necessary, being that they were two different professions. I was twenty-three years old and was trying to maintain a decent living for my sister and me.

Here at the law firm I was a receptionist known as Miss Angel Jacobs. I had my own desk, supplies, and space. I didn't have to share an office with Mr. Bennifeld's other two loud-mouthed employees, Kim and Porsha, which was a blessing. I didn't know what I had done to those two, but it was evident that they did not like me. That was fine with me, though, because truth be told, I hated to be around them.

I could tell there was a problem with the two of them and me, because every time I came through the door, there was the rolling of eyes or the smacking of lips. They didn't talk to me unless they absolutely had to. When they did speak to me, they gave me attitude.

My job was to see what a potential client's case was, look it up, and tell them the price. After they accepted or rejected the offer, I would either thank them for calling or schedule an appointment for them. Many times the clients would leave me their number for my personal use, and depending on their charge, I might give them a call back. When I say "depending on the charge," I mean whether it was a misdemeanor or a felony. A misdemeanor wasn't as severe as a felony and a felon was what I refused to deal with. Drug charges were my only exception, only because sometimes that was the only way they could get their money.

Although Mr. Bennifeld clearly was against us dating clients, we still did it. He told us if he ever discovered we were, he would fire us. As much as I needed my job, I also needed dick from time to time, and if I had to get it from the workplace, then so be it.

The very first date that I considered was with a man who was charged with multiple counts of drug trafficking. He was fine, with dark skin and dreads. He had an accent that I loved. He said it was because he was from Queens. Whatever it was, I enjoyed listening to him talk.

His name was Quincy, and he looked and smelled like money. It wasn't that I was a gold digger, because money didn't mean much to me, even though having money was definitely a plus. He was also a gentleman. He held doors, paid bills, and always made sure my pockets were right. We went on a few dates and spent a lot of time together. It was almost two months before we had sex or anything. I fully regretted ever sleeping with him, not because he was a horrible lover, but because I lost control when there was sex involved.

He had come over to my house because I was home alone and he wanted to keep me company. We ate, watched TV, and cuddled. I enjoyed his company. I saw my soul mate in him up until we had sex. It started out so lovely. It was almost as if we were making love. He was kissing and touching all the right places. Our sex was passionate at first, but when he decided to hit it from the back, things went downhill.

He turned me around, and I tooted my ass in the air. He slid inside and began thrusting slowly, and then he picked up pace. I was gripping the sheets, and then my hands dived under my pillow and I felt my machete. It seemed like I clocked out after that. I didn't know what triggered my anger, but for sure, I was angry.

Then he asked me to ride him. I did with no problem. I was riding his dick like a bike, and he was moaning with his eyes closed. I saw that face that I hated with a passion, and I snapped. I grabbed my machete and sliced his throat. Blood gushed out instantly, and he put his hands over his neck to stop the blood. I sliced his hands up. I continued riding him as his body jerked and twitched.

"Baby, are you cumming?" I asked when his body stopped moving. "I guess you came," I said as I got off him. I went to the window and looked out of it. I watched the rain drop from the sky and land on my windowpane. I looked back and laughed. He should have known better.

I hurried to clean up the mess. I had to pick up Crystal from the sitter's house in an hour. I put his body in a garbage bag, and then I put the whole thing in a large-sized suitcase. I pushed it down the stairs, and then I dragged it out to his car. He had left his keys on my counter, so I'd grabbed them on the way out. I popped his trunk and struggled to put him inside it.

After I finally accomplished that goal, I went back in and got my red leather gloves. I put them on, bolted out the door, and hopped in his car. I drove his car into the Chicago River. I jumped out before it went over the ledge. I walked about three blocks before I caught a taxi. I took my red gloves off before I flagged it down. I didn't need the taxi driver tracing anything back to me. The taxi dropped me off two blocks away from my house. After I paid the driver and the taxi was out of sight, I started my journey home.

When I got inside my house, I sat on my love seat and cried. I hadn't meant to harm him. In fact, I had really cared about him. I just didn't understand what made me do the things I did and then later regret them. It seemed like I had two different personalities. It was quite weird, because out of all the murders I was accused of, this was the only one I could remember.

I was sitting at my desk at the law firm, filing papers and answering calls, when something caught my attention. He was caramel brown, maybe five-six, had a low fade, and his muscular body was covered in Rocawear. He walked up to my desk and spoke.

"I'm here to see Mr. Bennifeld," he said with a deep Southern accent.

"Do you have an appointment?" I asked, never looking up at him.

"Yeah, my name is Clifton Moore."

"Okay, take a seat and I'll let him know you're here," I said as I looked him up and paged Mr. Bennifeld.

"Thanks, Miss Jacobs," he said with a smile that revealed his diamond grill. I figured either he was a brother in the streets or he was in the entertainment industry, because those were the only reasons he would be wearing a grill in his mouth.

Upon looking him up, I learned that he was twenty-eight and had been charged with illegal weapons, drug trafficking, and improper use. He was from Atlanta, and he had quite a history in the illegal business.

Mr. Bennifeld called me and told me to tell Clifton to come into his office. I did as I was told, and after he disappeared behind the door, the two females I couldn't stand came over to my desk.

"Girl, do you know who that was?" Kim asked. Kim was a loud ghetto female. She was the leader of the two. She always seemed to have an opinion when it wasn't needed. She said she didn't like me because I thought I was better than them, but I figured it was pure jealousy.

"No. Who was it?" I asked, guessing I had missed something.

"Clifton Moore! The heavyweight champion," Porsha answered while rolling her eyes, as if I should have known who he was. She was Kim's shadow. Always cosigning and tagging behind her. I was sure she had no real problem with me, but given that she didn't have her own identity, she had no choice but to act as if she did.

"Don't know him," I said as I continued filing paperwork.

They smacked their lips and headed back into their confined office. I decided to Google him. The information that popped up let me know that Mr. Moore was somebody to know. He was filthy rich and very popular, and I wondered why I had never heard of him. I grew curious.

He was in the office with Mr. Bennifeld for quite some time, and when he finally made his exit, I fell in lust. He was beyond sexy, and his swag was something to admire. The two ghetto tramps rushed out of their office, asking for autographs and pictures. He did both with no complaints. He cracked a small smile and said, "Bye," as he walked past my desk and out the door. I sat there wondering if I would ever see him again.

After my shift was over, I had just enough time to grab something to eat before going to get Crystal. I decided to dine alone at Chicago's Home of Chicken & Waffles over on King and Oakwood. I seated myself at a two-person table by the window. I ordered quickly once I decided to have chicken and macaroni with a lemonade.

I was sitting there peering out the window, daydreaming, when all of a sudden a familiar face brought my drink to me. It was Clifton from the law firm. He sat across from me and smiled, showing his grill. I cracked a smile too. I was flattered.

"Why, thank you," I said, grabbing my drink from him.

"No problem. If I would've known you was hungry, I would've took you somewhere to eat," he said. His accent was making me wet.

"We are somewhere eating." I chuckled.

"Naw, somewhere elegant," he replied.

I raised my brow. From the conversation, I got that he was into me, but I didn't want to be into him. I already knew how this would end, but I couldn't stop myself from wanting him.

He told me he was single and was looking for somebody to settle down with. He had a daughter and was friends with her mother. I grew jealous of how he could brag about his daughter. Here, I wouldn't know my daughter if she walked past me. I felt that she was in Chicago. I guessed she was so close that she was far.

He continued telling me about himself, and I was enjoying every bit of it. I told him about myself . . . well, everything I thought he should know. We sat and talked for an hour, and I was damn near late picking up my sister. We exchanged numbers, and he walked me to my car.

"This you?" he asked and laughed, obviously at my car.

"Yeah. What's wrong with it?" I answered in defense while getting in.

"Baby, we gon' have to get you some better wheels soon," he said and chuckled as he shut my door.

I shook my head. My car was in good shape, and I, for damn sure, wasn't rich. I started my car and rushed to go get Crystal.

My little sister often stayed in the hospital and had to take so many different medications every day. I always found myself going to check on her at least twice at night. I was just always thinking I'd lose her in her sleep. I prayed she would get better, but there was no telling if she would.

She attended Buckingham Special Education Center. Although she had only Down syndrome and a slew of anxiety attacks, the Board of Education felt that her conditions were too severe for her to attend a regular school and that she needed and deserved special attention. Taking care of her as if she were mine, all by myself, was a lot of work and was sometimes a bit overwhelming. Sometimes I just wanted to give up, but I couldn't handle seeing my sister in foster care. I mean, I would have had to do the same thing had I retained custody of my daughter.

I went to go sign her out, and then I headed to her classroom to get her. She had a huge smile on her face when she saw me. It made me smile. I helped her put on her jacket, and then we headed outside.

When we got home, I immediately made her do her homework. It was always something simple to do, but it was complex to her. She went to the kitchen table and began her work, while I went upstairs to shower. I kept replaying my conversation with Clifton and smiled. I really liked the little bit of him I knew.

As I took my shower, I let the warm water run over my body. I started thinking of all the men who had fallen victim to my cookie jar, as I liked to call it. I also thought of the events that had led up to me getting pregnant and losing my child. Some parts were clear as day to me, while others were still a blur. Whenever I reflected on the day, all I would remember was lying on the bed, screaming. No matter how hard I tried to remember the whole process, I would always come up with that one scene.

Chapter 2

It had been a long day at work, and I was beyond tired. I soaked my body in the tub for hours. Crystal was with my best friend, Tiffany. Tiffany was always okay with keeping her for a day or so. God knew I needed the break.

I decided to call Clifton. It had been a couple of weeks since we had exchanged numbers, and we had talked on the phone only once. He had called me a few times, but I had ignored all of his calls because I just didn't want him to get too into me. It was like I would date someone, and when I finally gave him some, he'd come up missing. No visits. No calls. I didn't know if it was because I got too attached or if my shit was that bad. Whatever the case was, it left me lonely.

He picked up after the third ring. It was loud in the background, wherever he was. I could tell he had an entourage with him.

"Long time no hear," he said with his deep, sexy voice.

"I know it's been a minute," I replied.

"You haven't been picking up my calls. I wonder why," he stated. I could tell he had walked into a secluded room, because the noise had started to die down.

"Well, I have been really busy and, you know . . . a little unavailable." That was the best line I could come up with.

"Really? Well, I want to see you soon. I'm in Miami right now, but I'll be in Chi-Town next week. Don't be unavailable," he added. I could tell he was smiling.

"I'll try," I said before hanging up.

It was a Saturday, and I was completely available. I requested time off at Vision Nightclub and the law firm was closed on weekends, so I decided that the club would be the best place for me to be. I called my girl Treecy up, because she was always down for going out. As expected, she wanted to go.

I had already taken a nice long bath, so my only task was to find something to put on. I got up off my bed and headed to my closet. As I opened the closet door, I noticed a small speck of blood on the wall next to the door. I figured it came from Crystal, so I made a mental note to clean it up once I returned.

I decided the tight-fitting black dress that hung in my closet would be perfect for the night. I would wear my lovely red pumps with it and would carry my red clutch. I tossed the dress on the bed, sat down next to it, and started to rub lotion on my body. After slipping into my dress, I glanced in my full-body mirror and noticed my panty lines showing through the dress. That was a dress code no-no. I decided not to wear any panties at all. I slipped the thong off and proceeded to put on my pumps. After everything appeared to be in place, I was ready to go.

Treecy picked me up what seemed like a few hours later. She was a physical therapist assistant, so she was living comfortably, making good money. We decided to go to Vision Nightclub, only because I bartended there and we could get discounted drinks.

When we arrived, we found a good parking spot down the street from the club, but we still had to walk at least a block to get there. The line of people was wrapped around the building. Now, Vision Nightclub had a majority white crowd. You would rarely see many blacks. I had to admit, the whites knew how to party and have a good time.

When we reached the door, the bouncer, Scott, let us go right in. We never had to pay, which was a good thing. The club was already packed, and the bright and flashy blinking lights made everyone appear to be moving in slow motion. We headed straight to the bar. My mouth was watering for Cîroc Red Berry. I told my girl Brittany, who was working at the bar, to give me a cup of that and a cup of orange juice to chase it. Treecy got two shots of Hennessy, and she threw them straight back.

I met Treecy a while back. She was Crystal's physical therapist after Crystal had a muscle spasm that locked her arm up. Since Treecy was the best at what she did, I had to give it to her for getting Crystal's arm back to normal after several weeks of range-of-motion exercises. In the looks department, Treecy was facially challenged, no question about that. She had a nice shape and flawless chocolate skin. Her short haircut was always done, and she was always dressed in nice attire. She was born and raised in California, and she moved here to Chicago to attend college.

My girl, Brittany kept the glasses of liquor coming, and we didn't hesitate in drinking them. After about four drinks, everything started to look the same. I decided to hit the dance floor. I tapped Treecy to get her attention. She put her drink down and leaned in toward me.

"I'm 'bout to head to the dance floor. You coming?" I asked Treecy in her ear.

"Naw, I'm going to stay here and finish these drinks."

I got up and made my way through the crowd to get a spot that wasn't overcrowded with people. They were playing one of my favorite jams, Black Eyed Peas' "My Humps." There were a lot of people dancing and having a good time, so I got in the middle of the dance floor and rocked my lumps. I spotted a few ladies on the dance floor who were dancing behind each other, humping each other. I tuned them out and partied like a rock star. After that song was over, the DJ played Rihanna's "Don't Stop the Music," and the crowd went wild.

As I was vibing and whipping my hair back and forth, I spotted a cute white guy. He was wearing a tuxedo. He stood about five-seven. He had perfectly tanned skin and dark hair. The blinking lights made it appear as though he was at a standstill, alone. The girl that I was, I started to make my way toward him. The room fell silent . . . well at least to my ears.

I could hear my pumps hit the dance floor. *Click. Clack.* They let out smoke, which messed up my vision. By the time I made it to where he was, he was gone. I turned in a circle, looking for him. He was nowhere in sight. I looked over toward the exit, and there he was, heading out

the door. I hurried over to the exit. There was
something about him that I wanted . . . or maybe
it was the drinks. When I finally got outside, he
was standing on the curb, flagging down a taxi.

I rushed over to him and grabbed his shoulder.
He turned around.

"Can I help you?" he asked in a proper tone of
voice.

"Um . . . yeah. Uh, you leaving?" I asked. I
didn't know what to say. Normally, I would
rehearse what I would say before I made an
approach, but not this time. I had been too damn
busy looking for him and hadn't had the chance.

"Yeah, I have an important meeting to attend
tomorrow morning," he stated with a smile.

"Oh, well . . . okay," I said, stepping back onto
the sidewalk.

"I'm going to the Palmer House Hilton on East
Monroe. I'll be sipping wine and lounging. You're
more than welcome to join me," he offered.

I smiled.

When the taxi pulled up, he opened the door
for me and I got in. He climbed in behind me,
and then we were on our way. I looked out the
window the entire drive there. I was daydreaming how this night was going to end. I couldn't
believe I had even got up the nerve to approach
this man. He must have read my mind, because

he knew I wanted to go with him. I decided to shoot Treecy a text telling her that I'd left early. She texted Okay, and we left it at that.

When we pulled up to the Hilton, I was in total awe. The hotel was luxurious on the outside, so I could only imagine what the inside would look like. Although Chicago was home for me, I had never been in this hotel. Mr. Tux paid the taxi driver and led me into the hotel. The inside was beautiful, and I couldn't stop myself from looking around. We got onto the elevator, and neither one of us said a thing. We knew what we were here for.

We were all the way at the top when we reached our floor. The large elevator doors opened, and we stepped off. There was only one door, and that one door was to the penthouse suite. He slid his key in the lock, and then we entered. The concrete floors let me know that we would not be doing anything on them. The spacious suite had chrome finishes and was decorated in black and white.

"You can have a seat," Mr. Tux said while going over to the kitchen.

I sat on the black love seat and rested my head on the plush white cotton pillow.

"You know, I never got your name," he said, smiling. He took his black tuxedo jacket off and laid it across a chair at the kitchen table. He went to the refrigerator to get a bottle of wine.

"Well, my name is Laya. Yours?"

"Josh. So do you always go to hotels with strangers?" He chuckled. He began pouring two glasses of wine.

"Actually, I don't," I said and giggled. He was sexy for a white guy. I was never really into white guys. I was wondering if he was the type to make the first move. If not, I was always down to do so.

He came over and sat down next to me, and then he placed my glass in front of me. I sipped slowly because I had had enough to drink at the club. After about four or five sips, I decided to sit my glass down and focus on him. My vision was beginning to blur. I scooted closer to him. Whenever I was drunk, sex was the only thing I was in the mood for, and I already knew I probably would never see Josh again. Honestly, it wasn't like I wanted to marry him or anything like that.

He placed his hand on my thigh, and the warmth of his hand there made me wet. I wanted so much more. I unbuckled his pants and pulled his dick out of those unattractive whitey tighties. He was kind of small, and he wasn't so thick, either, but I had already started, so I had to finish. I placed his dick in my mouth and began sucking it gently. The taste was somewhat salty, and maybe I should have made him wash it first, but I wasn't thinking. I started sucking it faster, letting the saliva drip from my mouth down his shaft.

He moaned loudly as he pressed his hand to the back of my head. He didn't pull my hair, like I would have preferred, and after about ten minutes of my amazing head game, I decided that he needed the real deal. He placed a LifeStyles over his dick, and I mounted him. There was something about riding a dick that put me on top of the world. He enjoyed the way I bounced up and down on him. I was sure he had never experienced sex like this.

I pulled him by the hair on the back of his head so that he could look me dead in the face. At that moment, I saw what I hated seeing. I let go of his hair. In my mind, I knew I had to move quickly. I kept riding while I searched the room with my eyes for something that I could use. When I saw nothing within my reach, I just grabbed his neck. I pressed my thumbs on his throat, causing him to change colors. He was choking.

He grabbed my wrists, gasping for air, but I continued to hold his throat. By the time I let go, his body lay there stiff.

"Did I put you to bed with this pussy, baby?" I asked while I still sat on top of him. I got up and rolled the condom off his dick. "He never even came," I said aloud while shaking my head.

I went to the bathroom to flush the condom down the toilet. When I was done, I took his pants and drawers from around his legs and threw them on the floor. I put his legs up on the couch and checked his pulse. . . . He still had one. I went over to the bed to get a cover so that I could cover him up. He was still alive, but he was so drunk that I doubted if he'd remember who I was tomorrow. As he remained lifeless, I took a quick shower, and then I cut up the towels that I had used, balled them up, and put them inside a big towel.

I kissed Josh good-bye, and then I made my exit. I saw a garbage chute by the elevator so I threw the towels in there before getting on the elevator. There wasn't anyone in the lobby besides the lady at the front desk. I didn't look her way. I left through the double doors to the outside world and flagged down a cab.

"Yes," I said, never looking up. One of the ditzy twins at work had called my name. I hoped it was work related, because we all knew there weren't any good vibes between us.

"We just wanted to know if you wanted to go out with us tonight."

I looked up at her and gave her a crazy look. It was Porsha. She was rocking the ugliest cheetah-print vest with some black slacks.

"I know we dislike each other, but we need to drop the unnecessary beef," Porsha stated with hope in her eyes. I didn't know if she was being genuine or trying to set me up. Them bitches were always up to something, so I stayed on my toes when it came to them.

"Go where?" I asked while I continued to focus on my assignment, marking appointments.

"Just to eat. We just want to kill the beef. I don't even know why we never liked each other to begin with."

I smacked my lips. She knew damn well they started the beef when Mr. Bennifeld gave me my own space. They'd been petty and jealous ever since. I agreed to go eat with them just to see how things would go.

We all decided to go to Connic's Pizza to eat after work. Porsha and Kim rode together, and I drove by myself. I didn't trust them enough to be carpooling. They pulled off before I did, and when they were out of sight, I decided to switch into my all-white Vans tennis shoes, even though they didn't look right with the coral skirt suit I was wearing. Luckily, they were the kind with no shoestrings, so it didn't look too tacky that I wasn't wearing any socks. I felt I needed to be on guard at all times with those two. I opened the back door of my car and slipped out of my coral pumps.

They were already seated with drinks at the table when I arrived. I walked over to the table they were at and sat in the booth next to Porsha.

Kim smiled. She was sitting directly across from me, and I could tell she was happy I came. "We ain't think you were going to come," she said and giggled. Her red silk shirt was tight. Her clothes always were. Kim just knew she was cute, but unfortunately, she was far from it. She seemed like she was down to earth and a fun person to be around. She just wasn't my type of person.

I chuckled. "Oh, my feet started hurting, so I had to stop and change shoes. That's why it took me a little while."

"Well, I'm glad you came." Porsha smiled. I figured she had never had a problem with me. She just didn't have her own identity, so she always followed Kim. Porsha was much prettier. She was model-figure tall and wore a healthy wrap in her hair. Her skin was cocoa brown and flawless.

"I'm glad I came too."

"Yeah, I hate us feuding and shit. You seem like a cool bitch," Kim confessed. She had a potty mouth. Every other word was a curse word.

Porsha nodded her head, cosigning as usual. I just shook my head. There really wasn't much to say.

The waitress came over.

"What can I get you to drink today?"

I ordered lemonade, as usual, and we all ordered a large pepperoni pizza. After the waitress left, we sat in complete silence for a good awkward ten minutes, until Porsha broke the ice.

"So, Angel, what do you do outside of work? You seem kinda quiet," she said as she twirled her straw in her cup.

"I'm a bartender at Vision Nightclub," I said, turning to her and looking her in the eyes. "You?" I asked.

"Shit, I like to party." She laughed, as if I should have known.

I cracked a small smile while I imagined what type of outfit she would come up with since her fashion sense had no sense. If she thought wearing anything like that vest she had on now was club worthy, then she needed to reevaluate herself.

"What about you, Kim? What you like?" I asked, turning my attention to her.

"I have a nine-year-old daughter, and that's what I do *most* of the time," she emphasized.

I nodded my head. I knew all too well what it was like to have to take care of a kid.

The waitress brought my drink and our pizza all on a tray. I watched her as she handled it with one hand. She set the tray on a stand and handed me my drink with a straw. As the waitress sat the pizza down on the table, I noticed Kim staring at me. I looked up at her, and she quickly turned her head. I didn't know if she was staring in admiration or if it was one of those up-to-no-good stares. I couldn't tell the difference, but I was hoping like hell she was admiring me, because I did not feel like whupping her ass.

I decided to go to the bathroom, so I excused myself from the table and headed to the back of the restaurant, where the bathroom was located. I stood over the plastic sink and sighed. Something about this get-together just didn't sit right with me. I couldn't prove that they were being shady. I had no evidence that they were up to anything, so I fixed my hair and headed back out to them.

Kim's head was down and Porsha's back was facing me when I got to the table.

"Girl, he want her out the game. He said that's why he sitting in jail now, for allegedly raping her. His own damn daughter," Porsha said, as if she didn't believe whoever the victim was, was in fact a victim at all.

When I got in her line of sight, she stopped talking about it and quickly changed the subject. It wasn't like I knew any of the characters in her story. I wondered why she didn't want to talk about it anymore. We didn't know any of the same people. I jumped on board and joined her new discussion about Kim's no-good man, Paul.

We ate, talked, and laughed the rest of the evening out. I was somewhat wishing we could have ended the beef a lot sooner. Still, my gut told me to stay on guard with these two. Since my gut was always right, I decided that I wouldn't allow myself to get so comfortable so soon with them.

Before we went our separate ways, we agreed to go out together that Friday.

Crystal's school had taken the second graders to a camp for kids with learning disabilities for the week. I needed the break. Hell, I needed every break I could get. It wasn't that I didn't want my sister. It was just that caring for her and knowing my child would be the same age was hard. I didn't know if my baby was dead or alive, and that killed me inside.

Clifton had asked me to meet him at the airport, and since I had nothing else to do, I took him up on the offer. It was chilly out, so I grabbed my black leather jacket and jogged down the stairs. When I reached the bottom, I noticed my red leather gloves sitting on the end table in the living room. I decided to take them, just in case it had gotten worse outside.

I locked the door behind me and hopped in my Taurus. I looked down at my navy blue leggings and black heels. I was cute and elegant, but now I realized why I was so cold. I was wearing spring gear. I decided to put my gloves on.

I pulled my visor down to look in the mirror. I noticed blood on both gloves. I instantly got paranoid. Where did this blood come from? I thought. I quickly took them off. It was necessary that I get rid of them. I didn't even know whose blood it was. I panicked, not knowing where I would ditch them, but knowing I needed to do so soon. I threw them on the armrest and started my car. I decided to just head to the airport and disregard my discovery, for now.

When I pulled up to the front entrance of the airport, there Clifton stood, looking so good. He was wearing a black Jordan sweat suit with the matching shoes. He had a Louis Vuitton suitcase in each hand. He was smiling from ear to ear when he saw me pull up. He didn't have his grill in. I doubted if all those diamonds in it would make it past the metal detector, anyway.

I parked my car and hurried out to help him put his luggage in the trunk. A few thirsty female fans rushed him, and as he talked to them, I opened the trunk. I decided to see if there was any room in my trunk for his stuff. When I opened up the trunk, I immediately closed it. There was blood in the trunk of my car. I stood there, trying to put these pieces together. I didn't know who or where the blood had come from, but I was determined to find out.

"Hey, you," Clifton hollered with a smile.

"Huh," I said, snapping out of my trance and looking in his direction. I smiled and walked up to him. He greeted me with open arms, and we embraced.

"My trunk is junky, so you can just put your bags in here," I instructed while opening the back door.

He did as I said and placed his heavy luggage on the backseat. After he was done with that, he got in the passenger's seat and we were off.

"So where are you going to stay while you're here?" I asked as I hopped on the highway. He smelled good and looked even better. I had to constantly remind myself to keep my mind out of the gutter, even though his presence made it hard for me.

"I thought with you," he said, sounding disappointed. I turned to him to see if he was serious. His facial expression told me that he was.

"Clifton—"

"Call me Cliff," he interrupted.

"Cliff, I would love for you to stay with me, *but* Mr. Bennifeld would fire my ass if he knew I was messing with you." As bad as I wanted him to stay with me, I knew he couldn't. He wasn't worth me losing my job.

"How is he going to know?" He chuckled.

I sat there wondering the same thing. He had a good point, because I had no intention of telling Kim or Porsha, and that would be the only way Mr. Bennifeld could find out.

"You have a point," I confessed.

He placed his hand on my thigh. "Baby, if you don't want me to stay with you, I could always get a hotel room," he stated.

I glanced at him. He was smiling. He was irresistible, and I wanted a piece of him. I smiled back. "That's not the case," I said.

I began to wonder if my house was clean and if it was even big enough for him. I knew he was used to the finer things, and I didn't have any of that. I hadn't expected him to want to stay at my house or even consider it.

"I'm just saying, we barely know each other, so I understand. I can get a room, and you can come stay with me some of the nights I'm here. I wouldn't mind if you stayed every night," he confessed.

I wondered what kept him so into me. We hardly knew anything about each other; we were not even close.

I smiled. He was winning me over. We decided that he would get a room and I would just stay with him. That seemed like the more logical thing to do, because I didn't know if he was crazy or what. Hell, I didn't know him.

He decided to stay at the Palmer House Hilton on East Monroe. The hotel looked very familiar, but I couldn't recall ever being there before. The valet took my keys, took Cliff's luggage out, and told me that he would park my car for me. The hospitality would definitely keep me here at the hotel. All the employees wanted us to do was check in and go to our room. They even handled the luggage for us.

Once inside the hotel, I gazed in amazement at the walls, the huge elevator doors, and the decor. It must have been déjà vu, because it felt like I had been here before. Who with was the question. After Cliff signed in and got the key to his room, we rode the elevator to the penthouse.

I told myself, *If this penthouse has black furniture with white pillows, then I know something.*

When we stepped off the elevator, there was one door, which I knew would be there. He walked up to the door and slid the key in. He opened the door, and there it was . . . the furniture I knew I would see. It was crazy, because I had been there before and had no clue who I been there with or when.

Chapter 3

"Take off your shoes and get comfortable," Cliff said. He went to get his luggage from the front desk of the hotel since they were taking too long to bring it up.

I went over to sit on the couch. I had a lot on my mind, trying to figure when I had been here. It was really beating me up inside, because I knew for a fact that I wasn't having déjà vu. This was definitely reality.

I slid my heels off and propped my feet up on the couch. When Cliff got back to the room, he sat next to me. He grabbed the white cotton pillow from under me and bopped me on the head with it.

"What's on your mind?" he asked.

I looked at him and smiled. He was so sexy. "What we eating?" I giggled.

"Room service, out to eat, each other. It doesn't matter," he responded while he grabbed my face and started kissing me. We shared a sweet, passionate kiss, and then, when we were done, we just sat there, staring into each other's eyes. I was really feeling Cliff, and I could tell that the feelings were mutual.

"I have to go to the restroom," I said seductively, excusing myself. Not only did I have to pee, but I also had to freshen myself up, in case he really was going to eat me. As I squatted above the toilet, I wondered what size his dick was. God knew I had no time for little johns.

While Angel was in the bathroom, preparing for whatever Cliff was going to give her, Cliff was on the phone, getting his plans in order. Stepping into the bedroom and closing the door behind him, he quickly called Porsha.

The phone rang twice before she answered loudly, "Hello."

"Yeah, it's Cliff. So I'm at the hotel with her, and I'm going to be with her for the whole week, so what is Albert trying to do?" he asked.

"Well, you know she's the reason for him doing his bid, and he's still pissed about that. He's to be released in the next month or so. I say just get closer to her so that she starts to trust you," she suggested, trying to make perfect sense. "I'm going to visit Albert on Wednesday after work. I'll let you know everything when I get back."

They said their good-byes, and then they hung up. Cliff really liked Angel, but her father was pissed at her for landing him in jail. He and Porsha had offered Cliff fifty grand just to get her to her father. Cliff didn't have to kill her or anything, just had to deliver her to him. Cliff loved money, but he loved easy money more than anything.

Albert Jacobs, Angel's father, was angry because he believed that Angel and her mother had accused him of raping Angel. The Feds had come to his job and had taken him into custody. He was the supervisor at a high-paying factory. They had done a DNA check, and it had turned out that they had enough proof to put him away.

They went to trial for three years, and the judge gave him five to ten years without credit for time served. He was all over the news and in every newspaper in Chicago. Throughout that time of humiliation, he even lost his job, his house, and his girlfriend, who left him and wouldn't have his back. He swore on his life that when he caught up to Angel, he would kill her.

He had never wanted her to begin with. Her mother, Teresa, had tried to trap him, because he was already in a relationship with his long-time girlfriend, Sarah. Teresa knew they were only creeping around, but she couldn't handle

being the other woman. He had kept Angel and
Teresa a secret for a very long time, until he was
taken into custody. Sarah came to the police
department with tears in her eyes, and she broke
it off and stormed out. She was his soul mate,
and he loved her dearly. Losing her made him
lose his mind.

After he was given his sentence, he was left
with nothing at all. He was pissed and determined to rebel. He knew it would take a while,
but he also knew that it would be well worth the
wait. He met a man named Paul while he was
in West Virginia, serving his time. Paul had a
girlfriend named Kim, who had a friend named
Porsha. The two girls would always ride with
each other to visit Paul, and since Albert never
got any visitors, they decided that Porsha, who
had no man, could visit and get to know him.

Albert was almost twenty years older than
Porsha, so his game was way above her head.
He would tell her a bunch of sweet nothings, put
his fingers in her pussy, and sometimes the cool
guard would let him fuck her in the bathroom.
She instantly fell in love with the prisoner.

On one particular day Kim and Porsha went
to visit their prison-bound loves and happened to
be complaining about how their coworker, Angel
Jacobs, thought she was better than everybody

else at the law firm. That name pissed Albert off. He told them to describe her, and they did. He knew in his heart that they were talking about his daughter. A lightbulb went on in his head. He had to use these bitches to his advantage, and that was exactly what he intended to do. He was going to use them to get to her.

He would tell the girls bits and pieces of how he ended up incarcerated, blaming Angel and her mother. Since the two girls couldn't stand Angel, they were convinced that every negative thing he said about her was true and that it was, indeed, lies that got him in prison. They couldn't understand why a father would molest his own flesh and blood, a child he barely knew. Albert didn't seem like that type of guy. He told them to befriend her and do whatever it took to get her to trust them. He put up fifty grand, which he would give to any man who could bring her to him. No killing needed, because he was going to handle that part.

Kim and Porsha saw the perfect opportunity when they noticed how Angel admired Cliff when he came to the office. He was down for the offer. Besides, in his mind, he wanted to fuck Angel. She was beautiful to him. Getting fifty grand for doing a little more than what he had planned was cool with him.

Albert kept his voice in Porsha's ear, reminding her that if she got the job done, he would marry her, because that showed her loyalty to him. Porsha hadn't had a man since high school. All she had ever got was occasional fucks from men. For a man to actually consider marrying her was a huge thing to her. She was sure the job would get done, even if she had to do it her damn self.

There were knocks at the bedroom door, causing Cliff to snap out of his daydreaming. He opened the door to find Angel dressed in nothing but her bra and panties.

"You ready for me?" he asked with a smile on his face. There was something about her that made him want more than just sex. He didn't know what it was, because he really didn't know shit about her.

He picked her up, placed her on the bed, and slowly slid her panties down. Angel lifted her ass up to help him get the job done faster, and he got them off, threw them on the floor, and then unsnapped her bra. She arched her back so that he could pull it all the way off. Once he did, he threw it on the floor, next to the panties.

He began nibbling on her breasts, sucking them and then blowing on them. That made her juices begin to flow, and it made her want him in her so much more. He started licking on her stomach, and then he covered it with kisses. After that, he started licking on her inner thighs. He stopped right before he reached her pussy. This was making Angel go crazy. More than anything, she hated being teased. When he felt as though he had teased her enough, he dived in.

He gently nibbled on her clit, slurped her juices, and then inserted two fingers at the same time. He twisted his fingers around in her while he sucked on her clit. Then he removed his fingers and replaced them with his tongue. Angel had her hand firmly on his head, her legs wrapped around his neck. She was inching up to the headboard, because his head game was just that good. After about five minutes of head, it was time to give her a piece of him. He reached into his pocket and pulled out a Magnum, ripped it open, and rolled the condom down on his dick. He swiped his dick between her pussy lips to get it wet, and then he slid it in slowly.

Angel arched her back and gripped the sheets, letting him know his dick was big. He stroked her slowly and gently because he didn't want to hurt her. To him, she was tight and soaking wet. Her insides were warm, and he could've fallen asleep in her. He sped up his pace a little. He didn't want to go too fast, afraid he might cum quickly. He wanted it to last as long as possible. As Angel closed her eyes, biting her bottom lip, Cliff filled her up, causing her juices to overflow.

When she finally opened her eyes and looked in his, she saw that face that haunted her. She began to panic. *What to do? What to do?* Before she could even think to react, Cliff pinned her arms down and continued to beat her pussy up. He was rough and she loved it, but she needed to get rid of him. Before she could think of what to do to get him off of her, she was beginning to cum. She started shaking and losing control of her body. She climaxed, and he came shortly after. He lay there on top of her, dripping with sweat, holding his body close to hers. In her head, Cliff was the man.

"Let's go shopping," Cliff suggested while we cuddled under each other. We had been chilling in the suite for three days and had done something interesting every single day. It was my weekend off of work, so I didn't have to worry about spending a minute away from him. I lifted my head up from his chest.

"Okay," I said. No way would I turn down the offer.

We both got up to take a shower together. It was a two-person shower with two showerheads, big enough for both of us. We both got in and washed each other. When I turned around for him to wash my back, he bent me over and shoved his dick in me. My eyes got big because his dick was way past normal, so it hurt a bit. He had one hand on my shoulder and the other one holding my butt cheeks open.

Fucking was definitely Cliff's thing, because he knew exactly how to handle me. After a few fast pumps, I begin to feel his tongue flicking across my clit. I was losing my mind, searching for something to hold on to. With nothing in my reach, I just grabbed my hair. I closed my eyes and opened them. I looked back as Cliff got up to put his dick back in me. Once again I saw that face. I stared him in the eyes, knowing I had to do something. He slid his dick in with ease and started pumping me slowly while staring me dead in the eyes.

Then I no longer saw the face I hated so much. I saw him, Cliff. He was sexy, and the way he bit his bottom lip while he looked in my eyes at the same time turned me on. I saw that face again, and I grabbed his neck. He started pumping me faster, and my tight grip loosened as my knees got weak and I felt myself about to collapse.

Cliff slid his dick out, picked me up, and lifted me up on his shoulders with my pussy smack dead in his face. He put me up against the wall, told me he wanted to taste my cum. He began eating me up. When I came for the second time, he placed me back on the floor, washed his dick off, grabbed a towel, and left me there as he exited the bathroom.

I stayed in there, washing myself completely, and then I turned the water off. I grabbed a towel and began drying off. I kept thinking about what had just occurred during our sexpisode. Why did I keep seeing *his* pathetic face? This had never happened to me before.

Cliff came in the bathroom fully dressed, laughing. "I swear women take forever," he said while shaking his head. He headed over to the sink to brush his teeth.

"Don't compare me to your other females." I dropped my towel on the toilet and walked out. I knew he was watching me.

I slipped on my black lace Victoria's Secret panties and bra after I sprinkled body mist all over myself. I had to make sure I smelled edible. I grabbed my red- and white-striped maxi dress out of my overnight bag. Once I got my clothes on, Cliff came into the bedroom and sat on the bed. He had on an outfit that was very similar to the one he wore the day I picked him up, except it was green.

"Sorry if I offended you," he said with sincerity. He watched me closely, almost as if he was studying me.

"Not offended. I just want you to allow me to make my own impressions." I was only being honest. I snapped on caramel wedge sandals and picked up the matching handbag. I also grabbed my short jeans jacket, in case it decided to get chilly. It was early October. Normally during this time of year, Chicago began to get much windier. However, today brought a nice cool breeze and sunny skies.

He nodded his head as if he agreed with me. He came up behind me and placed his arms around me and started kissing the back of my neck. After he released me, he grabbed my hand and led me out of the suite so that we could head to the mall.

Cliff's assistant and bodyguard met us at the front entrance of the hotel in an all-black Escalade. We both sat in the back, and then the driver pulled off. The driver was a dark-skinned guy who wore a lot of gold jewelry. He didn't say much, mentioning only the route we would take on our journey to Woodfield Mall, located on the outskirts of Chicago. During the drive there, Cliff kept reminding me that I could get whatever my heart desired. He told me the only limit I had was the one I put on myself. I smiled and made a mental note of that. I wondered if he would want something in return because he was treating me so good. *Is this how he treats all his lady friends?*

They had shut the mall down for the two of us, and it made me feel special. Our first stop in the mall was the Coach store. I had always wanted a pair of Coach sneakers. I had never really had the extra money to get a pair. Cliff sat in a chair in the middle of the store and let me shop away. When I was done there, I had two pairs of shoes, two handbags, and a pair of heels in my hand. He grabbed the bags from me and handed them to his bodyguard.

"You never have to hold anything when you're with a man," he whispered in my ear.

I looked at him and smiled. Our next stop was True Religion. I knew nothing about this clothing line, so I sat down on one of the seats, a stool. Cliff came over to me when he noticed I had sat down.

"What you doing?" he asked me.

"I've never heard of this store, so I don't think I want anything from here," I stated.

He smiled and shook his head. "Baby, this is something you want to have in your closet. I'll pick yo' shit out for you, then." He giggled. I shrugged my shoulders, giving him the okay, and then he walked off.

Then we went into a few other stores, and before long we had more than enough bags. On our way out of the mall, we spotted paparazzi snapping pictures of us. I got a little nervous, because I would hate for one of the magazines to reach Mr. Bennifeld's hands if my picture was in it. After we were safe in the car, Cliff nudged me.

"What's up, baby?"

"Nothing. I just don't want my boss to get a hold of any of those pictures they just took," I said.

"Don't worry." He put his hand on my thigh and began rubbing it. "If you get fired or if you simply want to quit, I'll take care of you," he said with firmness.

I looked into his eyes. I didn't trust niggas whatsoever. They were good at selling dreams, and I was thinking he was still high from my sex game. Maybe he was just talking.

"I'm serious," he said while grabbing my face and kissing me.

I simply said, "Okay," because I wasn't sure if he meant it or not.

Chapter 4

I placed my head on the pillow next to Cliff, and then I watched him sleep. I wondered what his intentions were. He was far too kind to me, and that was unusual in this day and age. I felt myself feeling him more and more as we spent time together, despite my suspicions. He was spoiling me and giving me whatever my heart desired. He was introducing me to the lifestyle I had always dreamed about.

It was his court day. I woke him up when the alarm clock went off at eight in the morning. He was due in the courtroom at nine o'clock sharp, and I had to be at work at the same time, so we both had to get up and get our day started.

We both got in the shower together. I watched the water drip from his muscular body as he scrubbed his face with the white washcloth. I washed my body in slow motion as I studied him. He was a sight to see. When he finished, I decided I was done too, so I stepped out with him. We dried off, and then I lotioned up as he powdered his balls. I chuckled. I found that cute.

"What?" he asked.

"Nothing. I just never seen anybody do that. Reminds me of a baby."

He laughed. "I don't want no sweaty-ass balls. It's mandatory," he explained while putting on his Sean John boxers.

When we were finally ready, I was dressed in a red blouse, black slacks that came to my knees, and my black pumps. Surprisingly, Cliff had on a black suit with red gators.

"Great minds think alike," Cliff said.

He wanted to drop me off at work and pick me up after my shift, but I couldn't risk getting caught.

"Just drop me off at my house, and I'll drive to work." I didn't want the two nosy bitches to be all up in my mix.

Arriving at work after being off for a few days was overwhelming. I wanted to go back to being under Cliff all day. Mr. Bennifeld stopped at my desk before he headed out to Cook County Courthouse.

"Hey, Angel," he said with his deep, stern voice. His voice was so deep that it was unattractive. Mr. Bennifeld was handsome, though. He was heavyset and had gray hair. He was happily married and had three daughters, all of whom he talked about on a regular basis.

"Yes, Mr. Bennifeld?" I looked up from the work I was doing.

"A guy by the name of Ashton Parker will be stopping in this morning. Please tell him to wait here for me. I shouldn't be long," he said as he put his trench coat on and headed for the door.

I wrote down the information he gave me on a sticky pad and stuck the note to my flat-screen computer monitor.

Kim came through the door shortly after Mr. Bennifeld left. "What's up?" she asked, walking toward her office.

"Not much." I started filing papers, waving her off a bit.

She stuck her head out the door. "Don't forget we're hitting the scene tonight," she reminded me. I was so glad she did because I had totally forgotten that I had even agreed to do anything with them. She must have read my face. She walked out of her office and over to my desk. She was looking pretty decent today, probably because her clothes weren't tight, like they usually were.

"You forgot, huh?" she asked.

I cracked a small smile. "Somewhat," I responded while giving her my attention. "What club?" I asked.

"Don't know yet, but I *do* know Angel is going." She smiled. She turned around to go back into her dungeon. Moments later Porsha came in, late as ever.

"Mr. Bennifeld here?" she asked me with a look of worry all over her face.

"No, he's at the court."

She sighed, letting me know that she was relieved. He had warned her time and time again about her tardiness, but to no avail, as she continued to be late.

I continued doing my work until *he* walked in. When the door opened and he entered, I smelled this scent that made me just want to eat him to pieces. I stopped what I was doing and looked up to see a fine stallion.

He looked like he was about twenty-one with his clean-cut face. He was rich chocolate, about five-five, had deep waves, and probably weighed one-fifty soaking wet. He was pretty slim, but size didn't matter to me, because his swag made up for the difference. He walked up to my desk as he took his Gucci frames off.

"I'm here to see Mr. Bennifeld," he said. He was very proper.

"Your name please?" I asked, standing up.

"Ashton Parker."

"Oh, okay. He's out right now, but he is expecting you. He told me to tell you that he'll be here shortly." I gave him the bedroom eyes. I already knew that if he showed me he wanted me in any way . . . then I was fucking him. I was obsessed with sex, and whenever I saw someone that I was sexually attracted to, I was determined to fuck him.

I watched him closely as he walked over to the chairs that were lined up against the wall. I resumed my work, but I could feel his eyes focused on me. Moments later Kim and Porsha came out of their office.

"Hey, we're going to grab something to eat. Want anything?" Porsha asked.

I shook my head no, and then they were out the door. Now I was alone with him. The only thing that was on my mind was getting a quickie, but I wouldn't dare make the first move.

"Is there a public bathroom?" he asked me.

I looked up and smiled. "Yeah. If you go through those double doors, it is over to the left. You can't miss it," I said.

"Can you show me? I'm bad with directions," he told me. He had the cutest puppy dog look on his face. I got up to escort him to the restroom. I was sure that he was up to something. I walked in front of him, and I was sure he was staring at my ass the whole time. My black slacks were pretty tight, so they made my ass poke out.

"Here it is," I said, pointing him toward the men's restroom.

He cracked a small smile, and then he grabbed my face and began kissing me. I started unbuckling his pants. I knew our time was limited. He returned the favor as he pushed the bathroom door open and locked it behind us. He pulled my pants and panties down, and then he set me on top of the sink.

He let his pants drop, and then he pulled his boxers down. He bent over and got a condom from the back pocket of his pants, and he ripped it open with his teeth. He took the condom out and handed it to me. I slid it down on his skinny dick, and then I massaged his balls.

"You want this, don't you?" he asked as if he didn't know.

I nodded my head, and I grabbed his dick and inserted it in my soaking wet pussy. He closed his eyes, and I whispered in his ear, "You have to make it fast."

He thrust fast and hard. He was so rough with me. He held my legs so far back that my ass was in the sink. There was no moaning. All you heard was his balls hitting my ass and my pussy farting.

He whispered while grabbing a handful of my hair, "You got some good pussy."

I grabbed his hand and removed it from my hair. I *was* at work. I wasn't receiving any pleasure, but I was glad I could accommodate him. He started slowing down while grinding his hips, and then it hit me. That face stared in my eyes, and my first reaction was to choke him, so I grabbed his neck firmly.

He grabbed my hands and broke my grip. "What the fuck is wrong with you? I ain't with that crazy, freaky shit." He pulled his dick out of me, and then that face disappeared.

Now I was looking at Ashton. I jumped from the sink and started putting my clothes back on. What had gotten into me?

He stood there staring at me, with his skinny dick still hard.

I wasn't myself. Why the hell was I fucking him at my job to begin with? Before I left the restroom, I turned to him while holding the door open with one hand.

"Mr. Bennifeld will be with you shortly."

When I got back to my desk, Mr. Bennifeld and Cliff were both in the lobby, talking. I sat down and pretended as if nothing had just happened. Shortly after, Ashton came from the restroom and sat down. Cliff looked at him and then at me as Mr. Bennifeld continued talking.

I know he suspected something was up, but he had no proof. I avoided giving him any eye contact.

"Hello. Mr. Bennifeld's law firm. Angel speaking. How may I direct your call?"

"What the fuck, Angel?" Cliff said on the other end of the phone. I didn't understand what he was tripping about, because, clearly, we weren't together. "What did y'all do?"

"Are you serious?" I asked him back. I must have had the I've-been-fucked look on my face.

"Your hair was messed up, and you looked suspicious," he explained.

I turned in circles in my chair as I listened to Cliff complain. My shift was almost over, and his mouth was the last thing I wanted to hear.

"When you get off, I want you to go straight home and then call me. I dare you to try and wash up before you call," was the last thing he said before there was a dial tone.

I looked at the phone, and then I set down the receiver. I wasn't sure if that was a threat or what. Whatever it was, it left me nervous. What was he planning to do?

I prayed that time would go by slowly as I cursed myself out for not washing up before I left the bathroom.

Mr. Bennifeld came into my office. "I have to pick my daughter up from school a little earlier today. It's fine if you want to leave early," he told me.

I wondered if I should tell Cliff that I was getting off early or not.

Kim, Porsha and I had made plans to hook up later that night. We laughed and joked on our way to the parking lot, happy be to going home. I got in my car and put the key in the ignition. When I started the car and looked up, I noticed the same truck that had taken me and Cliff shopping. *Is he stalking me?* Maybe I was tripping. He wasn't like that.

I headed straight home, and the first thing I did was relax on the couch. I hadn't been home for more than ten minutes at a time since Cliff had come to town. I kicked my heels off, unzipped my pants, and then kicked my feet up. I was restless.

I didn't think I smelled like sex, but you can never really smell your own stench. I looked at my grandfather clock and saw that I had forty-five minutes before I would technically be off work. I ran upstairs to shower.

I put the water at the perfect temperature, not too cold or too hot. I grabbed some underwear and quickly took my clothes off and hopped in the shower. I scrubbed my body clean with Dove soap. I was hoping that this would do the trick and that I wouldn't smell extra fresh when I got with him.

After about ten minutes of that, I turned off the water and stepped out. I dried off with my fluffy dry towel and wrapped it around me as I walked into my bedroom to lotion up. As I reached for my lotion on the top shelf in my closet, I came across something sharp.

"What the fuck?" I yelled. I had cut my index finger on something. I placed that blood-covered finger in my mouth, applying pressure to it. The taste of blood filled my mouth. I went to grab my vanity chair so I could see what had cut me. I continued to suck on my finger as I stood on the chair. There was a machete with blood on it shining on the shelf.

My eyes got big as a house. *First the gloves, then the trunk, and now this,* I thought. I had no clue where all this shit was coming from, but if I didn't know any better, I would think somebody was trying to set me up.

I stood there thinking about what to do and how to do it. I couldn't leave that machete sitting up there. Then again, I couldn't touch it, either. I also needed to clean my trunk and dispose of those gloves. There were so many unanswered questions going through my head.

I wrapped the machete up in my towel and put my chair back. I grabbed my first-aid kit so that I could clean and bandage my finger. I slowly started to put my work clothes back on, and then I jogged downstairs. I looked at my phone, which read 6:12 p.m. Normally around this time, I would be arriving home from work. I decided to call Cliff.

"What's up?" he answered.

"Home," I said. Then my phone lit up. I looked at it and it read CALL ENDED. So all of a sudden he wanted to be rude? I sat on the couch and waited for him to arrive.

It took about ten minutes before he was at my front door, ringing the doorbell. I quickly got up to open the door for him. When the door swung open, he was standing there with a weird look on his face. His eyes were glossy, and he looked deranged. He walked in without saying a word to me.

I closed the door behind him, and then he sat on my couch and patted the space next to him for me to sit beside him. I did.

We sat in silence for a few moments, and then he demanded, "Take those pants off."

I was thinking maybe he wanted to fuck me, so I did what he demanded without second-guessing him. I stood up and slid my pants and panties down. He stuck three of his fingers up my coochie, and then he took them out and sniffed them.

"Lay down," he demanded.

I was puzzled. I had no clue what this man was up to. I did what he told me, and then he pushed my legs open. He put his face between my legs and started licking my pussy. He lifted his head up and gave me an evil look, and then he nodded his head as he stood up.

"Get dressed," he told me. Then he sat back down.

I looked at him the whole time I was putting my clothes on. I didn't know who this man was at that moment. After my pants were up and buckled, Cliff hopped off the couch and began choking me. I grabbed his hands, trying to pry them off my neck, but to no avail. I prayed he wouldn't punch me, because I knew I would be knocked out. After all, he was a professional boxer. I gagged and lost my breath before he let go of my neck. When he finally did, he grabbed me by my hair.

"Lie to me or cheat on me again, Angel, and I'll kill you." He mugged me, and then he released the tight grasp he had on my hair.

I placed my hands on my sore neck, sliding to the floor. I didn't know when I became his girlfriend or why he was so obsessive all of a sudden, but I was scared straight. We had been kicking it for only a week, and he was already showing me his true colors. I didn't like the new him and had no intention of continuing our friendship.

"I think you should leave, Cliff," I said in a low tone.

He looked at me sideways and then chuckled. "Bitch, you fuck with me, you stuck with me." He got up and headed to the kitchen.

I couldn't believe my ears. I had no control over this situation, and it seemed as if I was trapped. I looked behind me into the kitchen, where he was. He had the refrigerator door wide open, and then he closed it and demanded that I come cook.

I did as I was told. I really didn't have any other choice. I didn't know what had triggered the sudden change in our friendship. Nor did I know when it had become a relationship, but whatever it was, it had me walking on eggshells. I was scared for my life, and now I felt like a child who was terrified of her father.

Chapter 5

"Did you not do a background check on him? I mean, you do have his files at your job, Angel. Damn!" Treecy was all in my ear about the Cliff incident. She and Tiffany were like my only friends. I figured she would understand my situation more than Tiff, so I told only her.

"No. I knew he was there for drug charges." I felt dumb for not taking it a step further by looking at all the things he had allegedly done.

"Girl, he's abusive! Just Google him," she said.

I got up from my bed and headed downstairs to my desktop. I turned it on and surfed the Web for information on Clifton Moore. The first thing that popped up about him was that he was an undefeated heavyweight champion. I scrolled down on the computer screen and read another link that stated: "Undefeated heavyweight champion Clifton Moore accused of domestic violence and assault on his longtime girlfriend Brittany Campbell."

I read the article, and by the time I was done, I realized that Cliff was a nutcase with a major anger problem. He didn't appear that way to me at first, but now the signs were crystal clear. Cliff had gone back home, down South, and I felt so free. He had been smothering me ever since that day. I swore to myself that I wasn't going to continue dealing with him.

My plan was to keep my word, until Mr. Bennifeld confronted me with a magazine in his hand. I thought nothing of it, until he stopped at my desk with an angry look on his face.

"What's this?" He slammed the magazine down on my desk. The front cover of the magazine had a photo of Cliff and me getting in the black truck with bags in our hands. It read CLIFF'S HOT NEW LOVER.

I was speechless.

"What did I tell you ladies? No talking or sleeping with clients. That's mixing business with pleasure, and I can't have that," he said while throwing the magazine away. "I'm sorry, Angel, but I have to let you go," he said. He looked at me and shook his head before he walked back into his office. Once inside, he gave me one final look of disgust, and then he shut his door.

I was hurt. It was like my heart had fallen though my chest. I was getting paid good money here at the law firm, and now I would have to kiss all of it good-bye. What were Crystal and I going to do?

Tears almost fell from my eyes, until I saw Porsha in her doorway, watching me like a hawk. She came over to be nosy and to help me pack my shit. I knew in her head she was celebrating, but fuck that bitch. Before I left, she gave me a tight hug and took my number. We both promised to stay in touch. I knew that wasn't going to happen.

After all of my belongings were in my backseat, I got in my car and drove off with no destination in mind. I rode around crying hard tears. I needed my job, and now all I had was the nightclub, and that wasn't bringing in enough money as a primary source.

The only thing I could think of was to call Cliff. He told me not to worry. He said he was making plans for me to move down to Atlanta very soon. He added that he would pay my bills this month. I had two choices: either I had to leave with him and let him take care of me or I had to come up with a way to make a living here in Chicago. That was something to ponder.

After we hung up, I decided I needed a stress reliever. I knew that nothing relieved stress for me more than some new dick. I headed over to happy hour to let loose at Grami's bar over on Grand Avenue. It was the afternoon, and I had a couple of hours before happy hour ended. I found a parking spot, parked my car, and turned off the ignition. I took one last look in the mirror. My face told a story of its own. I was stressed. I put my game face on and exited the car.

Inside, there weren't many people, but that was okay with me. I took a seat at the bar next to a young thug. He was accompanied by two other guys, and I listened in as they discussed the fact that he was coming up on a dice game.

I flagged down the bartender and ordered myself a Sex on the Beach. When she came back with my drink, I pulled my money out of my bra and started counting it out for her.

"I got it," the young thug said while scooting my hand out of the way so that I couldn't hand the bartender the money for my drink.

I looked at him and cracked a smile. He had caramel-colored skin and shoulder-length dreads, which he had up in a ponytail. He had a little accent, but I couldn't detect where he was from. He was rocking an orange and white Sean John outfit with some all-white Adidas.

He was cute. He also looked like he had just turned twenty-one, maybe. Being that I had come to this bar only for a quickie, age wasn't my concern. I put my money back in my bra and began sipping my drink through the straw.

"The name's Omar," he said.

"I'm Laya," I told him as I got up from my seat. "Thanks for the drink." I started walking away, and I already knew that I wanted him to fall victim to my goodies. I wanted him to chase me for them, so I headed over to the other side of the bar and placed my empty cup on the counter.

"You want something else?"

I turned around to see who this voice belonged to. It was Omar.

"Sure. Are you stalking me, Omar?" I chuckled.

"Hell, naw. I just wanted to make sure you was straight," he said as he handed me a fifty-dollar bill before he walked off.

I was impressed that he was impressed with me, or was he one of them crazy young stalker niggas?

I ordered a shot of Hennessy and threw it in the back of my throat. I wasn't a heavy drinker, so it never took much to get me drunk. After about four drinks, I was up looking for Omar. I found him in some short girl's face. I tapped him.

"Yeah?" He turned his attention to me.

"Come on," I said as if we had come together.

"Where to?" he wanted to know.

I grabbed his arm and led him out of the club. When we got outside, he stopped me.

"Where we going?" he asked again.

"You're coming with me. I'll bring you back when I'm done with you," I told him as I unlocked the doors to my car.

"You drunk? You don't wanna do this." He was still standing there.

"How do you know?"

"Because you're wasted and you don't need to be driving. Call me when you sober up, and if you still wanna fuck, then I'm down," he said. He walked up to me, took my phone from out of my bra, and put his number in my phone. He called his phone from my phone so that he could have my number, and then he handed my phone back to me. "Okay, I got your number. Go straight home, and I'm gon' call you in ten minutes to see if you cool," he said.

I put my feet in the car, and he closed the door for me. I was disappointed. I had come there with every intention of finding someone to have a quickie with, and I was leaving empty-handed. I was halfway to my house when Omar called.

"You cool?" he asked.

"Yeah, I'm almost home."

"Oh, okay. Well, call me when you get there. I'll swing by," he said, sounding sexy with that accent.

I hung up, thinking that maybe he just was afraid to ride with me. I pulled up to my house and almost forgot to put the car in park before taking the key out of the ignition. After doing that, I got out and headed to the front door. I barely got the door open. When I finally did, I stepped inside and then shut it behind me as I decided to lie down on the floor in front of it.

I looked at my phone to see what time it was. My BlackBerry read 1:45 p.m., and I had to go get Crystal at 4:30. I had to squeeze a nap in somewhere, so that was what I did, right there on the floor.

My nap was short and sweet. When I woke up, I looked at my phone. Two missed calls and it was 2:55. The two calls were from Omar, so I quickly called him back. I got up from the floor, and my head was doing 360s. I went to sit on the couch. After three rings, he answered.

"You okay?"

"Yeah, I'm cool. I fell asleep," I stated. I put my hand on my head as the room went round and round. I leaned back on the couch and closed my eyes. Those drinks had kicked in earlier than I had expected.

"So where do you stay?" he asked, getting straight to the point.

I gave him my exact address, and he told me he had to drop off his friend and then he'd be on his way. I decided to try to get up and brush my teeth. My phone rang, and I picked it up off of the couch and looked to see who it was. It was Cliff. I sighed.

Did I really want to answer this? I decided not to. I threw the phone back on the couch and headed upstairs. My head had slowed down from all the spinning, and I was starting to feel better. I heard the doorbell ring, and I hurried up and grabbed my toothbrush, put toothpaste on it, ran it under some water, and scrubbed my teeth and tongue. When I was done, I turned the water off and put the toothbrush on the counter. I wiped my mouth with my hand and headed downstairs.

I opened the door, and Omar was standing there, looking sexy. I stepped out of his way so that he could enter. He handed me some Motrin and walked past me and into the living room. I followed.

"How did you know I needed this?" I said with the tiny bottle of Motrin in my hand.

"I figured. I was watching you throw them drinks back." He chuckled.

I sat down next to him. "So you were watching me?"

He smile and nodded. "Just to make sure you was cool . . . not on no stalking shit," he explained.

I noticed that he had bedroom eyes, and that was exactly where I led him.

My legs were in the air, and Omar was beating the pussy up. He put my big toe in his mouth while putting my other leg on his shoulder. He flicked his finger across my clit and thrust his body all at once. Talk about multitasking. I knew he had to be young, because the way he handled me was like no other.

He slid his dick out and slid his tongue in. He twirled, slurped, and nibbled on me. I had a tight grip on the sheets, feeling like I could explode at any moment. He stuck his thumb in my ass while he still continued to eat me out. This was something new to me, and it made me feel so uncomfortable, but I didn't dare complain. He was under for what felt like forever before he came up for air, and when he did, he began kissing me. He slid his thick dick back in and continued humping on me.

He was crafted in the fucking game, and he treated this like an art. The positions he put me in were ones that I didn't know existed, and every grind, hump, and lick felt like it had been perfected. I kept getting the urge to choke him or to find something to bash his head with, but then something in me would say, *Calm down.*

There were a few times when I grabbed at his neck to choke him. Then I would end up pulling him close to me to kiss or to suck on his neck. I just wasn't myself while sexing him. It wasn't that I didn't like this new me, because I did.

When we were done, we held on to each other and I searched the bed for my phone.

"What you looking for?" Omar asked.

"My phone. I need the time."

"Almost four," he told me.

I got up and got in the shower. He came in and flushed the condom down the toilet and washed off his dick at my sink. Sex with him was so different. It was like I was a different person. I felt weird, but I liked it.

I found him pulling the sheets off of my bed when I got out of the shower.

"Where you want me to put these?" he asked while balling them up.

Yeah, Omar was way different from the rest. I had never pillow talked, nor had anyone taken my sheets off the bed for me.

"Just put them on the floor. I'll get 'em."

Omar had to go back to the block, but he promised that we would do something later. I wrapped my towel around me and walked him to the door. He kissed me on the forehead before he left, and I shut the door behind him.

I peeked out my window to see what kind of whip he was pushing. It was nothing special. He was driving a black Charger with no tinted windows and no rims. *They all can't ball,* I thought.

I ran up the stairs to get dressed, and then I ran back down to look for my phone. Finally, I found it on the couch. I grabbed my keys, and I was out the door and on my way to pick Crystal up from school. I decided I would tell Treecy about my new boo. When I went to dial her number, I saw that I had four missed calls from Cliff and a voice mail. I instantly called to see what he had to say.

"Look, Angel, I don't know what you call yourself doing, but if this has anything to do with that one incident between us, I'm sorry. I don't know what it is about you, but my feelings are growing and I really want us to be together. Give me a call."

I was confused. That situation had happened almost a month ago, and although we hadn't talked as much since then, I didn't see why he was bringing it up. He apologized a million times for it. He had told me he was drunk that night and, now that he had these feelings for me that he couldn't control.

I believed him. He hadn't put his hands on me since that incident, and I was happy that he wanted to take care of my sister and me. I just hated depending on people, because I liked having my own stuff. This good dick source that I had recently discovered . . . there was no way I could let it go.

I called Treecy, like I had intended to do in the first place, and I told her every detail there was to tell.

She just kept asking, "Are you for real?"

I asked myself that question, too, because that little boy wasn't *little* at all. "I lost my job too." I hadn't really faced the fact that it was gone up until now. What was I going to do?

"Damn them nosey-ass paparazzi bitches," she said.

I knew she felt bad for me, but she couldn't help me.

I pulled into Crystal's school parking lot. "I meant to tell you that Cliff wants me to go to ATL with him, but . . ." I paused.

"But you're not about to do that dumb shit . . . are you? He hit you once. He'll do it again," Treecy preached.

"All right, boo. I'm about to get Crystal. I'll call you when I get out of here." I didn't feel like hearing it, so I ended our call. I dreaded going to get my sister more than anything. They acted as if we were coming to get criminals. All the shit you had to go through. Signing them out, physically going in the class to get them, checking in at the desk once you got them, and *then* you could leave.

After the thirty minute process, we were out of the school and in the car.

"How was school?" I asked, looking at her in the backseat.

"Okay. I'm tired," she stated through yawns.

I smiled and shook my head. She was only eight, but she acted like she was grown.

After my mother was diagnosed with the cancer, she wasn't able to really take care of Crystal. Although she still had legal custody of her, she asked me to take care of her, because she didn't feel that she could care for her alone. I agreed. It didn't seem like my mother really liked her, anyway.

Crystal and I shared the same mother and father. Our mother was Teresa Gable, a teen mom who was looking for love in all the wrong places. She met my dad, Albert Jacobs, at a club that she had no business being at. He had a woman that he had been with for years. The woman's name was Sarah. My mother knew about her. She was just young and dumb, and she thought she could take him from Sarah. When my mother discovered she was pregnant with me, she just knew my dad would be all hers. Little did she know, having a child by him was the worst thing she could have done.

At first he showered her with gifts, sneaking her out of the house and spending time with her. When she got knocked up by him, she didn't hear from him until she delivered me. He would come by just to see what I looked like, and when he did, he felt I resembled him, yet he still wanted a blood test. When the results came back that I was certainly his, he started coming around a little more, but nowhere near enough. He didn't speak to me or anything when he came by. It was always at night when he surfaced. They would make me go to bed so he could fuck her, and then he'd be out like he was never there.

My mother would always shed tears because of him, not believing that she was the one to blame. She allowed him to walk all over her. She was overprotective of me at first, but a little after my sister was born, when I turned about fifteen, she started treating me like shit. It was weird because I didn't remember her even being pregnant with Crystal. I guess she hid it good.

My father went to jail soon after Crystal was born. I didn't know why, but I did know he had a long bid to do. I didn't know if he'd been released or if he was still incarcerated. Either way it went, I didn't give a damn, because he never gave a fuck about me or my sister. Hell, I wouldn't even know the man if I saw him.

When I got to the house, Crystal was asleep in the backseat. I carried her in and took her upstairs to her room. After I tucked her in bed, I decided to give our mom a call. After a few rings, she answered with an attitude.

"Yes, Angel?" she said through the phone.

"How you feeling, Teresa?" I gave her an attitude back.

"Good, and you? Have you been taking your meds like you're supposed to?" she asked. She was very concerned.

I just shook my head. I hated when she asked me about those damn pills. There wasn't anything wrong with me, so I didn't think I needed to take them. I honestly couldn't remember the last time I took them.

"I guess that's a no," she said.

"Mom, I don't need them."

"Angel, you have a problem, and you don't act normal without them. You *need* to take them," she instructed. "If you're not going to take them, send Crystal back."

"You're not in any condition to take care of her. You barely can take care of yourself." She must be crazy.

"And if you ain't taking them damn pills, then neither are you!" she yelled.

I pressed the END button on my phone. I was done listening to her fuss. I really didn't know why I had even called. We argued every single time we spoke. I went upstairs to get the pills that I should have been taking for almost eight years now. I opened the medicine cabinet in the bathroom and grabbed the bottles. Abilify and Lithium were prescribed to me years ago.

I was fifteen when I was diagnosed with this bullshit. I couldn't recall everything that led up to me being bipolar. Maybe I just didn't believe it. I mean, would you? No one knew about my diagnosis. Not even Tiffany. I felt they had no reason to. I hated for somebody to judge me. If they knew I was bipolar, every time I flipped out, they would assume it was the disorder taking its toll. Another reason was that I didn't think I had a problem.

I hadn't taken the medicine daily, like it was prescribed, in over ten years, and I was doing just fine. I hadn't harmed a soul, but I was the crazy one? I couldn't stand my mom for making me feel that I was going crazy all this time.

I opened both of the bottles and poured all the pills in the toilet. After both bottles were empty, I flushed the toilet. I wasn't going to take them, anyway, so there was no point in storing them in my medicine cabinet.

Chapter 6

Octavia, one of my friends, had thrown a party because her parents had gone out of town. Any drugs or bottle of liquor a teenager could want was there. At this time in my life, I was in love with Grey Goose and weed. I was drunk and high.

I never thought of myself as the prettiest girl, but the guys thought otherwise. I was light skinned and had shoulder-length hair. I stood five foot five inches, and had Chinky brown eyes. I was a stick figure. I weighed 110 pounds. When it came to fashion, I was a plain Jane type of girl.

Growing up as the only child for fifteen long years was lovely. My mother spoiled me with her love and attention. Although my father came over all the time, we never spoke. It didn't really bother me, because my mother made up for the loss. My father always wore a baseball cap and big sunglasses to cover his eyes, even in the winter. He was about six-two. He was very tall if you asked me, and he was a slender guy with a beer belly and a deep voice.

The last time I saw him was right before I went to Octavia's party. I was taking a nap, and when I woke up, he was leaving my room. I rubbed my eyes to make sure they weren't playing tricks on me, but he was already gone by then. I knew that before I fell asleep, I had been covered up. Now my covers were on the floor. I looked down at my pants, and they were a little crooked. I sat there in deep thought, wondering why things were in disarray. After looking at the clock and seeing that the party was about to start, I hopped out of bed and walked across the hall to the bathroom to freshen up. After I was done with that, I called Octavia to see how the party was doing.

When she picked up, it was very loud in the background. I heard music and people. "I was calling to see what was going on, but I can hear for myself," I said and giggled.

"Yeah, hurry up. Mike keep asking about you," she told me.

"Okay," I said before I hung up the phone.

I was already dressed, so all I had to do was tell my mom where I was headed. She was sitting on the couch, smoking a Newport, while my father was nowhere in sight. I told my mother that I was going over to Octavia's for a study party. For that reason, she said I could go.

My mother was a very pretty, light-skinned lady. She used to have a nice shape, but stress and life had made her lose her figure and damn near her mind. We weren't poor, didn't live in the hood or the projects. We lived comfortably. *Comfortably* meant that we could afford our lifestyle. We were like best friends at one point in time, until one day I started feeling like she hated my guts. I didn't know what I had done or even if I had done anything. I just learned to stay out of her way, and my life ran much smoother.

After she gave me permission to go, I called my friend Tiffany. She lived across the street from me, and we decided it was best that we walk to the party together. Tiffany was Mexican, and she was fast as can be when it came to boys. She was the youngest out of five girls, and I always thought she was trying to keep up with her sisters. She would tell me that she was still a virgin, but that was far from the truth. I let her think that I believed her, although she had to be a fool to think that. Either way it went, she was the closest thing I had to a best friend, so I never judged her.

After we hung up, we met each other outside. She was with her cousin, Nicole, so all three of us made our way to the party. I couldn't wait to get there and be with Mike. He wasn't my boyfriend, but he had taken my virginity, so he was valuable in my life.

"Girl, I know it's going to be some niggas up in there," Nicole said. I guess being boy crazy ran in their family.

"I ain't even thinking about a nigga. I'm trying to get high," Tiffany said. Tiffany and I had developed this obsession and a need for weed. We had tried it a few times with her sister Jamie before we got hooked on it.

Octavia opened the door with open arms. She was smiling from ear to ear as she gave each of us hugs. We smiled and then walked into her house. There were people everywhere. My eyes searched the house for Mike, and I found him cuddled up with Lindsey Price. I smacked my lips and rolled my eyes. I was ready to go already.

Tiffany grabbed my arm.

"Girl, fuck him. You ain't come here just for him, anyway," she said, making a lot of sense.

I sighed and shook my head, letting her know that she was right. Octavia stopped in front of us.

"Y'all want something to drink, a blunt, a seat?" She laughed.

We all followed her to the kitchen, where the drinks were being poured and served. I got a full glass of Goose. Nicole kept telling me that I was drinking too much, but under the circumstances, I needed it.

The whole night, Mike was all over Lindsey, like I wasn't even present. I was hurt and feeling sick, but I couldn't let them see me down. I went to the patio, where a few guys were smoking a blunt. I sat down so that they would know that I wanted to partake in what they were doing. One of the guys was Davon, a popular guy in school. He was Mike's best friend and was the running back for the school football team.

"You sure you want to hit this?" he asked. His light skin gleamed under the patio light. He was cute, but he wasn't quite my type. I nodded my head as he passed me the blunt. I inhaled it and exhaled it. I took one more hit before I passed it to the boy who sat to the right of me. Whatever kind of weed they were smoking, it was strong.

I instantly started feeling a little different. I was thinking of Mike and how he was better off dead, Lindsey too. The blunt made its way back to me, and I puffed it twice again, then passed it. My vision became a little cloudy, and I couldn't feel my hands. I decided that it was best that I went back into the party. I went to go find Tiffany. It seemed as if there were a million people there. I could hardly see their faces or hear their voices. I looked for Tiffany for about an hour before I decided to give up.

All of a sudden my bladder got full. I rushed up the stairs and into the bathroom. I barely got my shorts down, but I managed. I sat down, and it felt as if I had held my bladder for days. The urine just wouldn't stop coming out. When it finally stopped, I hurried and wiped myself. There was a loud thud on the bathroom door, startling me. I moved slowly as I stood up and pulled my panties and shorts up. Paranoid, I slowly walked up to the door. I was afraid to know who it was.

"Hey, hurry up! A nigga gotta piss." It was Mike's voice.

I calmed down and opened the door. He smiled as he pushed me back into the bathroom. He closed the door behind us, and I never said anything about what had happened earlier, although I wanted to. My mouth just couldn't let the words escape.

"You been smoking?" he asked while grabbing my face and staring into my eyes. I wanted to say yes, but I just couldn't. "Angel, have you been smoking?" he asked, repeating his question.

I managed to nod my head.

"With who? Not Davon, was it?"

Still, the words wouldn't come out, so I nodded again. I wanted so badly to speak, but it was like my mouth was glued shut. He threw the door open and ran down the stairs. I didn't know what was going on. The room was spinning, and I was in a standstill mode.

I closed my eyes and sat down. I couldn't stand this feeling much longer. Tiffany and Octavia came running up the stairs. They kept asking me if I was okay. I didn't see what all the fuss was about. All I did was smoke a blunt and drink some Goose. I did that all the time.

I couldn't answer them, nor could I move. I just felt my body press up against the bathroom floor, and I kept my eyes closed. I heard Octavia tell Tiffany that Davon had laced the weed. It was like she was saying I had gotten a Mickey slipped to me. My brain couldn't register all of what she was saying. I stopped caring about what she was talking about.

They picked me up off the floor and carried me into Octavia's room. They put me in the bed, left me there, and shut the door. Lying there, I kept seeing dragons fly across the room. I was scared for my life. I gripped the covers tightly. Moments later the door was flung open and in walked Mike. He sat down on the bed. He began rubbing my hair while shaking his head. He kept telling me that I was going to be okay and that he would always love me. I continued to watch the dragons fly.

He began kissing me and touching me. I remembered him repeatedly saying he was sorry. I started kissing him back, holding his face. I was horny as ever. I pulled his shirt over his head, and then he stopped me.

"Naw, Angel, I can't," he told me. I ignored what he was saying and continued trying to take his shirt off. "No, baby, you're not in your right mind," he said as he kissed my hands. I couldn't understand why he didn't want to fuck me. I thought he loved me. I tried my hardest to curse him out, but the words wouldn't leave my mouth.

He stood up and started walking toward the door. He stopped with his hand on the knob, and then he looked back at me. He told me he loved me and that he was so sorry and that he would pray for me. Then he walked out.

I continued to lie in the bed, horny as ever. If Mike didn't want to fuck me, I was sure somebody else did. I tried getting up, but I couldn't get the strength to lift my head from the pillow. While I was struggling to get up, Davon walked in.

"Look, Angel, I apologize for not telling you that I laced my weed," he said while walking up to the bed. I didn't hear a word he said. The only thing I heard was, "Angel, I want to fuck you." The closer he got, the more I wanted to fuck him.

When he was within my reach, I grabbed him and began kissing him. At first he pulled away, but after a while he began kissing me back. He started unzipping my shorts, and I took his shirt off. It was weird how I got all my strength back when I was about to have sex. It was like I was powerful again.

He pulled his basketball shorts down, and then out came his dick. He fiddled in his pocket, and then he pulled out a LifeStyles condom. He bit it open and took the condom from the package. Before I knew it, my panties and shorts were off. I spread my legs, and Davon got in between them. He slid his small dick inside of me and began to pump me fast. He reminded me of a rabbit. As I lay there laughing, I could tell I was making him mad.

He stopped fucking me. "What the fuck so funny?" he asked.

"You and this little-ass dick." I laughed even harder.

He put his hand around my neck and began choking me. I grabbed his hand, trying to get him to let go, but it wasn't working.

"Laugh now, bitch," he said as he gripped my neck tighter. I couldn't get a word out, and I could barely breathe. Davon was still fucking me, and now it was rougher. It started to hurt, and there was nothing that I could do about it. I could see that the dragons were still flying in the room, and then suddenly the room got pitch-dark.

When I woke up, I heard my mother going off about why she didn't like me going places. She complained that she didn't understand the choices I'd made in my life. She said if I kept it up, I would be a strung-out junkie. I looked around and realized that I was at home in my bed. I sat up and rubbed my eyes so that I could see things more clearly.

My mom was on the phone when she saw that I had woken up, and she quickly hung up with whomever it was she was talking to.

"I should really beat your ass, Angel," she said, giving me an attitude.

I rolled my eyes. My body was in too much pain to hear any nagging, and I was not about to listen to it.

"Don't roll ya damn eyes at me, girl. You know you done got slipped a Mickey *and* choked the fuck up with yo' dumb ass," she spat. I didn't know what the hell she was talking about, and I assumed she didn't know, either.

I rolled my eyes again and got up out of bed. I went straight across the hall to the bathroom. I stood in the mirror and saw purple handprints on my neck. I put my hand on my neck, touching one of the handprints lightly. It hurt a bit. My mom was standing in the doorway, talking even more shit.

"You don't remember that, do you? Nasty little bitch," she stated while she started walking away.

I poked my head through the doorway and looked at the back side of her in disgust. My mom never talked to me like this, and it hurt me to hear her speak to me this way. I walked back to my room with my head down. I didn't see why she was treating me like that. I decided to call Mike, because I missed him and hadn't seen him in a few days. I listened to the phone ring three times before he picked up.

"You cool?" Mike asked when he picked up.

"What? Yeah, I'm cool. What do you mean?" I didn't know what he was talking about.

"You know, the weed thing? Davon? The whole ordeal at the party?" he said, trying to remind me.

Honestly, I didn't know what he was talking about. "Mike, what are you talking about?" I was completely puzzled. I played with the telephone cord. I was clueless and was dying to know what the fuck everybody was talking about.

"Angel, nothing. I'll talk to you in school tomorrow," he said, rushing me off the phone.

Before I could even respond, I heard the dial tone. I put the phone back on the receiver. I placed my head back on the pillow. I closed my eyes tightly, and then I opened them. When I opened them back up, I saw dragons flying around. I quickly shut my eyes again.

My hands started losing feeling, and my head started spinning. I tried sitting up, but I couldn't. I wanted to scream for my mom, but I couldn't get the words to come out. Tears started falling from my eyes. What was happening to me?

The next day in school, all I saw was funny faces. Everybody was looking at me sideways, and I didn't like the shit one bit. I didn't say anything, though. I saw Tiffany at her locker and decided to approach her. I walked up behind her.

"What's up, Tiff?"

She turned around with a look of concern on her face and put her hand on my shoulder. "Are you cool, *chica?*" she asked.

"Why does everybody keep asking me that shit? Yes, I'm cool," I said. I was starting to become annoyed. I was irritated as hell.

Tiffany grabbed her books from her locker, and then we walked to our drama class together. She sat down in a front seat, and I made my way to the back, where my assigned seat was. Everyone was looking at me crazy. Some were grinning and whispering, while others were just looking at me.

I didn't get what the big deal was, and I was beyond tired of the glares, so I spoke up. "What the fuck is y'all staring at?" I spat. I stared down the whole class.

Nobody uttered a word. They all turned to face the front of the class. Our drama teacher, Mrs. Kyle, walked in moments later and began our lecture.

Thirty minutes into the class, I started seeing dragons flying. This time they looked like they were trying to attack me. I kept scooting my chair farther and farther back, until I was up against the wall. I didn't know where everyone in class went, but I was in a dungeon alone . . . or so I thought. The biggest green dragon stood right in front of me. I covered my eyes and screamed. I heard giggles but saw no one. I could feel its hot breath on my leg. I was so scared. I got out of my seat and ran for the door.

I turned to look back, and the dragon was right on my heels.

"Please, don't kill me," I cried while trying to open the door. The dragon spat fire, making the doorknob hot. I quickly moved my hand and blew on it. I was sure it had burnt me. I heard Mrs. Kyle calling my name, but I couldn't see anyone.

I backed up into a corner as the dragon walked up to me, and sat down there with my hands guarding me. The dragon's breath was so hot on me that I began to sweat. I heard my name again but still saw no one. I felt hands on my shoulders and someone shaking me.

"Angel, what's wrong?" Mrs. Kyle's voice said.

I couldn't talk. My mouth wouldn't move.

"Honey, are you okay?" she asked.

Finally, I could see her. Now I could see the entire class, and everyone was looking at me like I was crazy. I was so embarrassed. The dragons were gone, and I was back in my classroom. Mrs. Kyle and I decided that it was best that I go see the nurse. The walk to the nurse was longer than usual. Every step I took, it seemed like the hall got longer and longer. I stopped walking and closed my eyes tightly, thinking that things would go back to normal when I opened them. When I opened my eyes, there was the dragon staring in my face. I quickly started running down the hall. People were looking at me, wondering why I was running full speed.

When I finally made it to the nurse's room, I saw Tiffany sitting in there, talking to the nurse. When they saw that I was in the doorway, they stopped talking. I already knew they were talking about me. They were way too obvious. Tiffany got up from the wooden chair and told me to call her as she walked past me and out the door. The nurse, Mrs. Laurel, told me to take a seat where Tiffany had sat. I sat down and looked around.

She sat down across from me and grabbed my hand. She held it gently and stared me in the eyes. I stared back at her, wondering when she was going to get this show on the road. I didn't want to be here all day. She let go of my hand. Her cheeks got red. She placed her long blond hair behind her ears and began her speech.

"Well, Angel, Tiffany has told me that you had an incident at a party recently."

I rolled my eyes. What was Tiffany doing coming in here, talking about me with this bitch? I sighed and turned my body so that I was no longer facing the nurse. Since she thought she knew everything, what did she need my input for?

"Okay, I see you don't want to talk, which is fine, but I do think you need to see a psychologist," she said as she stood up to find the referral paper. When she retrieved it, she handed it to me. She told me she had called my mother and that I had to wait in her office until my mother came to get me. I was beyond irritated.

My mother came in twenty minutes later. It looked like she had been crying. I wondered why. She told me to grab my stuff, and I did. I handed her the referral paper. She looked at it and sniffed the snot that had formed in her nose from crying. She hugged me, and then we left.

Chapter 7

"So tell me a little about yourself," the doctor said. I was lying on a leather chaise in a calm room. There was the sound of water and a cool breeze flowing through the room. I felt at ease.

"My name is Angel Jacobs. I'm fourteen, and I go to Lincoln Park High School. I'm a freshman there. I'm an only child, and I live at home with my mom," was all I said. He was writing everything I told him down on a notepad.

"Okay, Angel. Do you remember the party you went to a few weeks ago?" he asked me while he pushed his glasses back, closer to his face. He was a black man who appeared to be in his forties.

"All I remember is . . . going to the party with my two friends. I know there were a lot of people there. I remember having sex with Mike and that's it." I tried my hardest to remember the party, but it had become a blur to me. I couldn't get my mind to recap the events.

"You slept with Mike? Is that what you said?" he asked. It sounded like he was giving me a second chance to get it right. I couldn't think of me doing it with anyone else. It had to be Mike.

We sat there in complete silence. I kept trying to replay the party, but bits and pieces were missing. Davon suddenly popped up in my head, but I didn't know what he had to do with anything.

"Miss Jacobs, who all do you remember being at the party besides you, Mike, and the friends you went with?"

"Well, it was Octavia's party, so she was there. Um . . . Davon was there, and . . . I can't really think of anyone else." I covered my eyes. I wanted to cry. My memory was out the window. "I'm sorry. I just can't remember anything," I cried.

He looked at me and smiled a little. He took his glasses off and got out of his seat. He told me he had to discuss a few things with my mother. I cried, wondering when and why all of this was happening to me.

On the way home, my mom drove with both hands on the steering wheel, sniffling and wiping the tears from her eyes every so often. We didn't speak. We didn't say anything to each other. I just looked out the window and listened to the music that sang through the radio.

When we got in the house, my mother told me to take a seat on the couch. She wanted to discuss a few things with me. I sat down as I'd been told. I was eager to know what it was that she wanted to discuss. I needed as many answers as I could get. She sat down next to me, facing me. She put her hand on my leg and shook it a little.

"Baby, now there's a lot going on with you right now. They think someone slipped some Mickey Finn to you at Octavia's party. They aren't sure if it was ecstasy or crystals, but they're sure it was something. Whatever it might have been, it can cause you to hallucinate and have behavioral problems." She started welling up with tears. "This is something you'll have to deal with for the rest of your life. I scheduled you a doctor's appointment next week so we can find out exactly what's wrong with you and what's in your system," she sighed. "I've told your ass time and time again not to smoke with those little boys. Angel, them ma'fuckas don't give a damn about you! You need to start making wiser decisions." She got up and left me looking dumb.

I just sat there, soaking in everything she had just told me. I wondered who slipped me a Mickey. I didn't even remember smoking anything. I decided to call Tiffany. I got up and went to the kitchen, where the house phone hung on the wall.

"Hey, Angel," she said cheerfully.

"Hey. Um . . . do you remember who I smoked with at that party?" I asked, hoping she knew. I rested my arms on the counter. I could tell she was debating if she wanted to tell me or not, because it took her a while to respond.

"I think they said it was Davon and his boys. I'm not certain," she answered, trying to clear things up.

"Oh, all right."

"You coming back to school?" she asked me. Ever since the day I was sent to the nurse's office I hadn't been in school. They said they wanted to know exactly what was wrong with me first before they allowed me to come back. They said I was a disturbance and that I was dangerous to the other students.

That was a bunch of bullshit. They were a danger to me. Were it not for one of their students, I wouldn't be having all these problems. I decided not to even answer her question. I just hung up the phone. I figured if she saw me in class, she'd know I was back. If not, then I wasn't.

My mother was behind me when I turned around from hanging up the phone. I jumped because I wasn't expecting her to be there. "You scared me," I said.

"Whatever. Don't call that bitch again," she demanded as she walked away from me.

***

"So the weed was definitely laced with ecstasy. What this means for Angel is that she now has a disorder. It's what we call bipolar disorder," the female doctor told my mom. "I'm going to have to place her on medication for this." She handed my mother the prescription paperwork. "Be sure she takes it as directed. If she *doesn't,* things could get a little rocky," she added. "She will be a force to be reckoned with, and she can begin hallucinating. So you see how severe this thing can be."

My mom sat still in the chair, only nodding her head. You could tell from the look on her face that she was hurt by the situation. I was too. I just didn't see anything wrong with me; except for the fact that I saw dragons here and there, I felt normal.

I knew that once I left the doctor's office, I wasn't taking no damn pills and that was final! That doctor clearly didn't know what the hell she was talking about. Bipolar people were crazy, and I was nowhere near crazy. I sat on the table quietly, shaking, ready to slap the spit out of that doctor's mouth. That bitch was the crazy one.

After the doctor said all she had to say, she left the room.

My mother stood up and walked over to me "You heard what she said, Angel," she said, seeing if I was paying attention.

"Yeah, but I ain't buying that. Ain't nothing wrong with me." I just knew my mother didn't believe that shit.

She gave me the look that told me she did.

"You think I have a problem, Ma?" I asked.

"Angel, you're not the same. That's all I'm going to say." She told me to put my clothes back on so that we could leave.

That hurt bad. My own mother thought I was crazy. How could she? Why would she? I slowly put my clothes back on and started to walk out of the examination room with my head hung low.

As my mother grabbed the doorknob to open the door, the doctor came in. "Angel, there's a little more information that I need to give you," she said while looking at a chart. "After running through all the tests, I also found that Angel is five weeks pregnant."

"Excuse me?" was my mother's response. She was at a loss for words, and so was I. I didn't even remember having sex with anybody except for Mike.

"Yes, she's pregnant. The dates match up to the time of the party," the doctor added while looking at me with concern all over her face. I really couldn't register the things that she was saying.

I honestly didn't believe shit the doctor had to say. I didn't even think she was a real doctor. My mother stood there teary-eyed. Obviously, she believed everything the bitch had to say, but why? Because she had a degree? That didn't mean shit.

"It looks like Angel is getting agitated," she said while looking at me.

My mother looked at me, puzzled. She grabbed my hand and held it tight. I stared at her. Who was she? She didn't look like my mom. I got paranoid.

My thoughts told me that they were going to try to hurt me. I tried to free my hand, but the more I tried, the tighter her grip got. I looked around the room, and there I was, in that same dungeon I was in when I was at school. I knew this shit wasn't right. I wasn't supposed to think like this, but I couldn't help it.

I tried my hardest to get loose from her grip, but it was damn near impossible. She grabbed a hold of me, and I just started to scream. I heard the doctor say, "We need help!" but I didn't know if it was to help attack me or to prevent me from being attacked. Tears welled up in my eyes when I saw the dragons coming toward me.

"Please don't kill me," I cried as I continued to try to break free of my mother's grasp. I heard my mother's voice, but the lady didn't look anything like her. She was a dragon with a human body. I closed my eyes, and when I opened them, I was sitting in the corner of the doctor's office.

People were staring at me and whispering. Kids were all over the place. Some were crying, while others were laughing. My mom's face told me she was embarrassed and worried. I didn't know what had come over me. From that day on, I had to take two different kinds of pills every day. I hated it. I used to spit them out in the garbage or act as if I was taking them, but my mother picked up on that early in the game. After she discovered I wasn't really taking my pills, she would make me take them in front of her and she wouldn't leave until they were down my throat.

I had so many doctor appointments a week; plus, I had to see a psychiatrist twice a week. I was banned from my school and now had to be homeschooled. The whole bipolar lifestyle pissed me off. I couldn't do anything without my mother being there.

At one particular doctor's appointment, I had to get a pap smear. My mother stayed in there with me the entire time. I grew uncomfortable.

After the procedure, my primary physician, Dr. Gunner, came in and asked me if I was aware that I was eight weeks pregnant.

"Do you know who the father is?" Dr. Gunner asked me.

"I don't even recall sleeping with anybody," I told her. I was being totally honest, and I needed her to believe me. She nodded her head and wrote some things down.

"Now, Gunner, don't mistake me for no ho! 'Cause I'm not one," I said, rolling my eyes. For all I knew, she could've written "Patient is a ho" on that pad of hers.

"No, no, Angel. I just put down that you didn't remember who it could be," she tried to explain, as if that wasn't describing a ho in a nice way.

"Never did I tell you that I didn't remember who it was. I told yo' ass I didn't remember doing it at all. Don't twist my fucking words up!" I yelled. I hopped down from the table, ready to whup her judgmental ass.

My mother grabbed me and told me to calm down. Dr. Gunner rushed out the door. That was her best bet, because I didn't like being judged. Now I had to figure out whose dick was so horrible that I forgot we slept together. My mother kept trying to remind me that they had already told me I was pregnant. I couldn't recall

anyone telling me anything about a pregnancy.
I simply told her to just shut up and mind her
business. She gasped and got quiet.

This was too much information given to me at
once. Here I was, a kid my damn self, and now I
was going to have one of my own. I didn't have
the slightest idea who could be the father of this
baby growing in me. Maybe Dr. Gunner was
right. Maybe I was a ho.

Chapter 8

There was chaos throughout my entire pregnancy. I was beyond tired of everything and everybody. Most of all, I was irritated with the appointments, the vitamins, and even the creams that would prevent me from having stretch marks. I had a reason to complain all the time. I didn't want this baby, but my mother didn't believe in abortions.

I didn't see why she would want an innocent kid to grow up without a father. She should be able to see the pain it was creating just by looking at me. My pleas fell on deaf ears, because she didn't care how much I begged. Getting an abortion just wasn't an option. It just wasn't happening.

One particular day my mother was gossiping with Miss Cheryl from down the street. Now, this lady knew everybody's business and didn't have a problem telling the next neighbor about it. She was also on the neighborhood block watch committee, so you already knew she knew any and everything that went on.

I had just woken up from one of my many naps, and I was on my way down the stairs to get some milk, which I was craving. My mother and Miss Cheryl were in the living room talking when I heard, "Yeah, Angel's trifling ass doesn't even know who her baby daddy is. You know I think she was fucking my man."

I couldn't believe my ears. Who the hell was her man? If I wasn't mistaken, she hadn't had male company in years. I crept down the stairs slowly so that I could hear them better.

"Really? You think she would do that?" Miss Cheryl was trying to milk my mom for all the information.

"You think she wouldn't? Hell, I seen him coming out of her room one too many times," my mother announced.

I gasped. Who was she talking about? Nobody ever came out of my room, and I didn't have the balls to fuck in her house. By this time I was at the bottom of the stairs and could see the back of both their heads. They were sitting on the long sofa that faced the door.

My mother looked at her and said, "The only reason I'm making the little bitch have that baby is to see if it's his." She looked at Miss. Cheryl. "And if it is . . . that bitch gotta go!"

Miss Cheryl gave her the "Are you serious?" look, and my mom returned it with an "I'm for real" smirk. "Girl, don't be like that," Miss Cheryl said. I guess she was as shocked as I was.

"Like what? That bitch made me lose my man and took him. The only reason that nigga came over here it seemed like was for her. He fucking her, and all I got was to give him head. Fuck the ungrateful bastard," my mother vented.

I had heard more than enough. I ran back up the stairs as tears filled my eyes. They must have heard the stairs creak, because Miss Cheryl was at the bottom of the stairs, asking if I was okay.

I heard my mom say, "Don't baby that bitch." Then I shut and locked the bathroom door.

A voice started talking to me. It said, "Just do it, Angel. It's not like anybody's going to care." I opened the medicine cabinet, took both of my bottles of pills, and filled up the cup on the sink counter with water. Then the voice came back to say, "What are you waiting for? It's obvious that you're better dead than alive."

Tears began to form in my eyes, and I answered back. "You're right." I took half of both bottles. I didn't feel any different. I had expected to pass out right after. I went into my room and grabbed my deceased grandfather's machete, which sat on a top shelf of my closet. I had it put up in a box, and after knocking everything down, I retrieved it. I took a hair ribbon and tied it around my arm tightly. I stood up and focused my eyes on my wrist. When my vein was poking out, I sliced it. Blood gushed out and flowed down my leg and on the carpet. I fell on the floor.

The pain was sharp, and my vision started to turn black. I couldn't see anything, and then I could no longer feel anything. I was at ease.

"Glad to have you back," a female voice said.

I turned my head in the direction the voice had come from. It was a dark-skinned lady in a hospital scrub, writing in a folder. I looked around the room and realized that I was lying in a hospital bed. I started touching all over my body, and I felt all kinds of tubes. I sat up and started pulling the tubes out of myself. The lady came over and tried to make me lie down.

"No, no, Miss Jacobs. You don't want to do that," she said.

I ignored her and hopped off the bed.

"Miss Jacobs, listen . . . ," she yelled.

I turned around to face her.

"Look, you tried killing yourself, and you have been out of it for quite some time now. You really need to lie back down, because you won't make it," she claimed as she began walking up to me.

I stood there, eyeing her. I didn't know if I should or shouldn't believe the shit she was saying. I climbed back into bed and lay down, and she started reattaching the tubes to me. She told me that she would be back with my dinner and asked me to just remain calm. She told me her name was Janet and that she would be my nurse for the next six hours.

The room was cold and clean. The only thing I could hear was the medicine dripping in the IV. There was a little square TV hanging from the ceiling and the remote was on my call light. I looked around the room. There were no get-well-soon balloons, flowers, or cards, or any other sign that someone loved me.

Out of nowhere, I felt a sharp pain in my wrist. I looked down to see what it was, and I saw that my wrist was bandaged up. I peeled the tape and took the bandage off. My wrist was stitched up and had dry blood all around the stitches. I decided that my only option was to turn the TV on. I had nothing else to do. I flicked it to the Lifetime channel. There was some movie on about a man stalking his ex-wife. I could barely hear anything that they were saying on the screen, but it was better listening to that than the sound of the IV.

I had been in the hospital for almost two weeks, and they were treating me like a convict. Every five minutes there was a hospital employee of some kind who would come in just to check on me. I couldn't even piss in peace.

Janet was checking my vitals and telling me about her son, who was offered a scholarship to Ohio State University. I was listening, not really giving a damn, but I acted as if I did.

"So you do know you're twenty-nine weeks pregnant?" she began.

"Pregnant?" I said with disgust. I had a small paunch. I didn't look pregnant, though.

She gave me with a puzzled look. "You didn't know you were pregnant?" she asked while wrapping the blood pressure band around my right arm.

I shook my head no. She gave me the "Yeah, right" look and I went off. "Look, Janet, don't start giving me looks like I'm a liar. What the fuck I gotta lie to you for? Huh? You ain't my damn mama," I said as I snatched my arm from her.

"No, Angel. It's just that we were told that you were aware," she tried to explain.

I just rolled my eyes. I was done with her and her lies. My biggest pet peeve was someone judging me, and she was doing just that. She left the room shortly after I let her take my blood pressure.

When she walked out, Mike came in. I instantly grew angry. I hadn't seen him in God knew how long, and here he was, trying to creep back into my life. He had his head down as he walked over to sit down on the swivel chair. We both sat there silently. He was looking handsome in his Nike starter outfit with the matching shoes. I just stared at him with an evil look while he stared at the TV. I knew he couldn't hear it, because I couldn't.

"You need to quit fronting," I said to him, breaking the ice.

"Look, I heard what happened to you, and I'm real sorry," he confessed. He stood up and walked over to my bed. "You're just not the same anymore," he said.

I just sat there and listened, because I had no clue what this man was talking about. I was the same, and nothing had happened to me. "I don't know what you're talking about, but I'm pregnant," I told him.

He looked surprised. "By who?" he asked.

Wrong question.

"What do you mean, by who?" I questioned him. I was itching to smack the stupidity out of him.

"Angel, you don't think that this baby is mine, do you?" he asked with a dumbfounded look on his face.

"Who else's could it be? You're the only person I've ever had sex with." I couldn't believe that Mike was in doubt about this.

"We haven't done anything in almost a year. It can't be my baby."

I was fuming with fire, and every word of denial that slid from his mouth pissed me off. He was still talking about how and why he couldn't be the father, and I just snapped. I grabbed him by the neck and began shaking him. I had a grip so tight that there was no way air was sneaking through. He was coughing and turning red, but I just enjoyed watching him struggle.

Luckily, Janet came in at that moment to check on me. She was the only thing that kept him alive, because I was going to kill him. She ran over to the bed and grabbed my hands, but she couldn't pry me off of him. Then she came back and stuck me in the side with a needle. I slowly loosened my grip, and then I drifted away.

Chapter 9

"What you say your name was?" asked the little eighteen-year-old I met while buying a quarter of weed.

I had gone downhill since I lost my job. It had been damn near a month, and my depending on Cliff was coming to an end. Omar and I were still fucking around, and he was always good for breaking me off with a few hundred dollars here and there. Cliff had introduced me to a lifestyle that the money Omar gave helped me keep up.

"Does it matter?" I asked in my seductive voice. I put his dick in my mouth. We had just got done smoking a blunt, and with him asking me a whole lot of worthless questions, he was blowing my high. I began licking his shaft and then twirling my tongue around the head of his dick nice and slow.

"N-n-no, it d-d-don't," he answered.

I noticed that I had him where I wanted him. We were lying on the floor of his sister's apartment, and it made me feel fifteen all over again. I didn't really mind, because it gave me a thrill. After teasing him and getting his dick rock hard, I began jacking him off while nibbling on his earlobe. Then I started sucking and blowing on his neck. His dick started thumping, and I knew for sure he was vulnerable.

"You ready for this pussy?" I whispered in his ear. I was still jacking him, and to add fuel to the flames, I started massaging his balls. All he could do was nod his head, but that was enough for me. I reached into his pocket to get a condom out, and he snapped out of his trance.

"What you doing?" he asked, moving my hand. I felt two condoms and a bankroll.

"Getting a condom. Damn!" I acted as if I was irritated as I snatched my hand out of his hand and sat up. I folded my arms and rolled my eyes.

He, too, sat up and wrapped his arms around me. "Baby, don't trip. I just don't let *nobody* go in my pockets," he explained, handing the condom to me.

I cracked a smile, as if he won me over. I grabbed the condom, opened it, and slid it down his long, thick muscle. I had a plan, and now it was time to execute it.

I slid my body down on his dick and began riding him like a bull. I placed my hands on his chest and thrust my hips up and down. He held my hips so tight, his nails pierced my skin. I began rolling my hips as I heard that slushy sound I loved so much. He moaned and groaned, and his eyes were nowhere to be found, because they were in the back of his head. I kept the pace constant, and then when Mike's face appeared it blew my high.

"Ugh, why won't you leave me the fuck alone!" I yelled.

Eighteen was so deep in me, and he wasn't paying me any attention. I grabbed a pillow and put it over his face. I put all my weight on it, and he fought until he lay there, lifeless.

"You stupid, ungrateful bitch! How dare you keep her from me, Mike? You fucking bastard," I screamed as I punched the pillow and cried. I cried as I continued riding him.

Eventually I collapsed on him, rested my head on the pillow, which still sat on his face. I wrapped his arms around me, and then I fell asleep. My heart was broken. I loved Mike dearly, and here he was, keeping our daughter from me. When I woke up, I realized that I had slept for over two hours. I looked around the room, wondering where the hell I was. I looked down and noticed I was lying on some man. *What the fuck?* I thought. I eased up off of him.

He was knocked out cold. His pants were on the floor, and his money was seeping out. I looked at him and then back at the money, then back at him. He seemed to be in a deep sleep. I tiptoed over to his pants, and when I got to them, I kneeled down and slowly eased the money out of his pockets. I looked back at him, and that was when I noticed I was buck-ass naked. I carefully looked around the room for my clothes.

After I found them, I slipped into them quickly. I snatched the pillow from the man's face. He was cute and young, and I had to be fiending for some dick, because I definitely wasn't a cougar. I left my panties right by his head, just in case his memory was off like mine.

On my way out the door, I noticed half of a blunt on a stand. I decided to grab that too. I had put him to bed, so in my mind he owed me one. I shut the door quietly and then headed to my car. On my way I noticed a lady who resembled the little boy a lot. They had the same eyes. As I was walking to my car, she ran up the stairs that I had just come down, and went into the apartment I had just left. When I was halfway to my car, I heard a loud scream and then, "He's dead! He's dead!"

That was my cue to get the hell up out of there. I hopped in my Taurus and put the pedal to the metal. I instantly got the chills as I drove home. *He's dead! He's dead!* kept replaying in my head. I couldn't go home. I started to remember those gloves and the crap in my trunk. Damn! I needed to get rid of this shit.

I rode all the way to the outskirts of Chicago and parked my car where no one could see me. I got out and popped my trunk. The smell was so deadly that I almost passed out. I already knew the only way to get rid of this was to get rid of the car altogether. I didn't want to get rid of my only form of transportation. I knew that if I just drove it into the water, they would still be able to check the DNA and trace everything back to me. I decided to take the tags off, set the trunk on fire, and then drive the car into the water.

I removed my tags, closed the trunk quickly, and got in to drive to the nearest store. The nearest store wasn't near at all. In fact it was too damn far. I walked into the convenience store and went straight to the back, where the lighter fluid usually would be. I got a few stares from the customers, and that was when I realized I was in an all-white neighborhood. I already had the lighter fluid in my hand, and in my head it was too late to put it down. I slowly walked to the counter, and next thing I knew, the guy from the club walked in. I never thought I would see him again, and when he saw me, his eyes got big and he started backing up. He eventually backed up all the way to the door. He was frightened.

"You are a crazy bitch!" he yelled with his hands up. He was basically telling me to stay back. I didn't know what the hell this man was talking about.

"What?" I was disgusted that he was embarrassing me. All the white customers were already skeptical about me. Everyone watched the show that he put on.

"Oh, don't act like you don't remember, *Laya,*" he said.

I was confused. *Who the hell is Laya?*

"I'm sorry. You must have me mixed up with someone else. My name is Angel," I assured him.

"So you don't remember going to the Palmer House with me after the club? You don't remember me . . . Josh? You don't remember damn near killing me? Psycho cunt!"

I put the lighter fluid on the counter. The cashier collected my money, all the while giving me a crazy look. He handed me my bag, and I began walking out. I rushed past Josh and quickly got in my car. I heard someone say, "Get her plates." But I was too embarrassed to care. After all, I had plans of getting rid of my plates after I left the store. I sped off and continued on my mission.

I parked my car at my designated place and hopped out. I popped my trunk and looked to see if my mini toolbox was still in there. I found it under a few of my clothes. I took the screwdriver out and began removing my plates. I moved fast, looking over my shoulder, making sure no one was watching me.

I was paranoid as hell and happy that I was able to get the plates off. I threw them in the trunk and poured the lighter fluid all over the trunk. Then I lit a match and threw it in. I quickly ran to the driver's side, started the car, and put it in neutral. I backed away from the car and watched it slowly go over the rail and into the water. I began walking slowly in the direction I had come from.

I started thinking about the whole ordeal at the store. Did I really leave the club with that guy? I wasn't even that type of girl. Why would I ever try to kill him? He seemed harmless. It dawned on me that the hotel had looked familiar to me. Maybe I did go there with him. I just couldn't see myself trying to kill anyone. I wasn't crazy . . . *or was I?*

I walked all the way home. When I got inside, I turned on the radio in the kitchen, tuning it to a local news station. "Once again we have breaking news. There was a nineteen ninety-six Ford

Taurus set on fire and blazing in the Chicago River. Officials believed that this was an act of arson. Police have still not identified who the car belonged to. We'll have more at eleven," the reporter said.

I sat on my kitchen floor, rubbing Concrete. My heart dropped. Although I had already expected all of this to happen, it still hit me like a ton of bricks. I sat there wondering if I had made the right move. Maybe I should have reported the car stolen, and then I wouldn't be in any trouble. *No wait,* I thought. *I'm not even in trouble. Well, at least not yet.* My mind was rambling.

I was scared straight. Now I was jobless and carless. I still had the bartending job, but being that I barely went, it was hard for me to get on the schedule as a full-time employee. I really didn't want to call Cliff for help. Omar was an option, but I just hated having to depend on people. The only thing I could think of was to start dancing. Although I didn't want to, I needed to. I didn't want to go live with Cliff or have to keep asking Omar for shit. I wasn't no damn charity case. Hell, I had to use what I had to get what I wanted, and money was definitely the motive.

I got up off the floor and decided to take Concrete back out to her doghouse. When I came back in, Omar was sitting on the couch with Crystal. I started to curse her out because she didn't know him at all and it was against the rules to let strangers in.

"Crystal, go upstairs," I ordered.

She smacked her lips and rolled her eyes and did as I told her. I was shocked that she even did all of that. It was so unlike her, but I brushed it off and went to sit next to Omar.

"So we're just popping up now, huh?" I laughed.

He pulled me closer to him and then put his arm around me. "Yeah, because somebody don't know how to answer their phone," he replied as he started kissing me on my neck.

I really enjoyed being with Omar. When I was with him, I was a different person. "Well, if you really wanna know, my phone is dead," I said, not really knowing why I didn't get his call.

"Well, if you really wanna know, I missed you." He started kissing me in the mouth and rubbing me all over. I knew we couldn't do much while my sister was here, wide awake. I told him to just wait until I put her to sleep. So I went upstairs to do just that.

When I reached the top of the stairs, Cliff called.

Answer or no?

I waited until I got into Crystal's room before I answered his call. He complained that he hadn't heard from me in a while and that he really missed me. He begged to come see me the following week. With Treecy constantly in my ear, telling me to leave his abusive ass alone, I really didn't want to see him. I told him that I would think about it, and then I hung up. He called back and left a message. I was too busy and on a mission, so I decided to leave my phone upstairs once Crystal finally fell asleep.

I stared at her and saw how much she looked like me. Our parents had strong genes, because she was the spitting image of me. I had noticed that lately she wasn't acting as slow as usual. She was actually kind of normal to me. Then again, I didn't know anyone else personally who had Down syndrome to ascertain how those afflicted with it were supposed to act.

After reading her one too many books, she was fast asleep. I jogged back down the stairs to get some dick. It was much needed, since it would help me get my mind off of that car and Josh ordeal. When I got downstairs, Omar stood in is boxers.

"Great minds think alike," I said while taking my shirt off and throwing it on his head. He laughed and then threw it to the floor. I took my pajama shorts and panties off and tossed them off to the side.

Omar came up to me, picked me up, put me on his shoulders, and began eating me out. It was almost as if he was French-kissing my pussy the way his tongue and lips moved. We were up against the wall, and I was searching for something to grab. After ten minutes of that pleasure, he let me down and I ran upstairs.

"Where you going?" he yelled from the bottom of the stairs. I ignored him and grabbed my sex toolbox from out of the bottom drawer of my dresser. When I got back downstairs, I found Omar sitting on the couch with his head leaned back. He was patient and fine.

"What's that?" he said as he lifted his head up.

"It's my toolbox." I sat it down on the coffee table and opened it up. Inside were sex oils, a dildo, a vibrator, sex cards, and sex dice. He went through and looked at everything and pulled out the dice.

"Let's play," he said while grabbing the two dice and rolling them on the floor. One said LICK, and the other one said BELOW THE WAIST. He opened my legs and began licking my inner thighs. I wanted so badly for him to give some more head. It became clear to me that he wanted to tease me.

I decided to roll the dice, and one said SUCK and the other one said BELOW THE WAIST.

"We know what that is." Omar laughed.

I smiled because only two things were suck-able below the waist, and those were his dick and his toes, and I for damn sure wasn't fucking with no feet.

I grabbed him by the dick and pulled him toward me. He crawled on his knees in my direction. He stopped in front of me, and I went in my toolbox and grabbed my throat-numbing spray and went to work. I placed his dick in my mouth and almost swallowed it whole. Omar grabbed the back of my neck and helped me bob my head. I couldn't feel shit, and that gave me the ability to put his dick all the way down my throat.

He released little moans and groans, but when he said my name, I knew I had him where I wanted him. He grabbed my face and slid his dick out of my mouth. "Wait. Wait. I don't wanna come yet," he begged. He slid me down onto the floor and grabbed his shorts. He took out his condom and slid it on, then came back between my legs. He reached over and went in my toolbox, and he pulled out the dildo.

"Let me see what you can do with this," he said.

He slid it into my already dripping wet pussy and turned it on. The head rotated and vibrated, making me squeal. I was grinding my hips up as if I was fucking a real dick. I had my hand wrapped around Omar's dick and was moving my palm up and down. He went into the toolbox and poured some sex oil on his dick, making the hand job go a little bit smoother. He put his head back, and I grabbed his hand and began sucking on his index and middle finger.

"All right, you got me wanting to get inside you," he said, turning the dildo off and placing it on the coffee table.

He slid his dick inside of me and began pumping away. As he fucked me like never before, a voice began to talk to me.

I know you're not going to let your noth-ing-ass baby daddy just get off that easy. I saw Mike in Omar, but then I didn't. I tried to tune the voice out, and after a while I didn't hear it anymore. I really didn't get to enjoy the sex, because I was too busy fighting the urge to hurt him.

I thought, *Maybe I am crazy.*

Chapter 10

"Turn that damn TV down!" I was beyond irritated. I had told this little girl twice about the volume being so high.

Crystal had the TV so loud that I could barely think. Porsha had called and had asked if I wanted to join her and Kim for some drinks. I'd agreed. I was still on cloud nine from the sex I had had with Omar the night before, so I was in a good mood.

Cliff was blowing my phone up, wondering why I was avoiding him, but with Omar in my life, Cliff wasn't really needed. Omar had paid my bills this month and hadn't asked for anything in return, while Cliff refused to pay for anything unless I devoted myself to him. My relationship with Omar had no strings attached, and Cliff wanted nothing but attachments. I really saw a different me whenever I was with Omar, and that was what I enjoyed.

I decided that Crystal needed to feel my presence. She needed to know that I wasn't playing with her when I said, "Turn the damn TV down." I went in her room to find that she was drawing a picture at her desk with Nickelodeon on the TV, which she wasn't even watching.

"Crystal," I called. She stopped drawing and looked at me sideways. "Little girl, please don't do all that. Now, turn the TV down or off. Choice is yours."

She nodded her head and got up to turn the TV off. Then she looked at me and smiled. "Happy now?" she asked sarcastically. I was blown away. She had got this horrible attitude from the sky. She used to be the sweetest little girl, and now she had become very disobedient.

I sat on her bed. "What's your issue?" I asked.

She picked up the chair that was at her desk and turned it to face me. She sat down on it. "I'm tired of you treating me like I have a problem, and not to mention, you're never around. This shit is for the birds." She gave me the attitude of a mad black woman.

"Crystal, you *do* have a problem," I reminded her.

"Girl, *you* have a problem," she said, pointing at me, "but I don't have one. Your mom made me act slow when those people was doing that study on me."

I was caught off guard. What did she mean by my mother *made* her?

"Excuse me?"

"Yeah, your mom made me act dumb so that she could get a check for me. She told me that if I wanted to eat and have a roof over my head, then I would do it . . . so I did," she confessed.

I was so irritated by the whole fact that my mom would even stoop that low and make my sister play like she was dumb. She had to attend a school for the special children all because of this.

"And why do you keep saying she's my mom? She's your mom too."

"Well, she told me that I wasn't none of hers and that she hated seeing me, because it reminded her how much of a mistake she made," she said, looking down at her lap. I could tell that it still had an effect on her.

I was completely lost at this point. I didn't know that all of this was going on when I moved out of my mother's house. I told her to tell me everything that had gone on in that house. She told me that from the day I moved out, my mother was cruel to her and would always say that she was stuck taking care of another bitch's kid. She would tell Crystal how much she hated her and how she would never amount to anything because she was born "a sin."

Crystal was five years old when I moved out, so I couldn't grasp the reason why my mother would talk to her the way she said she had. She was way too young. Everything she told me made me feel sick to my stomach. Instantly I grew upset.

"I never told to you because she said you didn't want me, either, and that's why you left me with her," she said with tears in her eyes.

I grabbed her and gave her a tight hug. I loved my younger sister, and I didn't want her to think anything different.

She told me that our father had raped her. He would always sneak in her room and touch on her and make her do the same to him. She mentioned that Mom knew but failed to do anything about it. My mother always played the dumbfounded role whenever my dad did something wrong. It seemed like she accepted his bullshit so that she could be a part of his life. My stomach turned again as Crystal continued to tell me how terrible her life was when I left. There was so much going on at that house that I had no clue about. I knew if I confronted my mother that she would deny it. My father was in prison, and I knew for damn sure he wouldn't admit to any of it.

I left her in her room so that she could continue drawing. I went to my room, and I called Tiffany. I told her everything my sister had told me, and she didn't sound so surprised by the news.

"I mean, your mom was always crazy, if you ask me," she blurted. I rolled my eyes. Tiffany had always been outspoken. "Don't get me wrong. She was cool, just a little off her rocker," she added.

I changed subjects and asked if she could keep an eye on Crystal while I went for drinks with my coworkers.

"I thought y'all didn't like each other," she said.

"For a while we didn't. Now, everybody is tryin'a end the beef," I responded.

She left it at that and agreed to keep Crystal.

Since I didn't have a car, Tiffany came and got Crystal for me. After Crystal was gone, I ran up the stairs and started to get dressed. There were a few knocks at the door. Porsha was coming to pick me up, and I hadn't told her my address yet, so I knew it couldn't be her.

I walked down the stairs with caution, wondering who it could be. I looked out the peephole, and there stood two police officers. One was short and chubby, and the other was tall and skinny. They were complete opposites, but they were both Caucasian. I turned around and pressed my back up against the door.

I was scared.

I decided I had no choice but to answer the door, so I did. I opened the door with a fake smile.

"Yes, Officers?" I said, trying to sound nice.

"Yes. Is Angel Jacobs here?" the short, chubby one asked.

"I'm her," I said. I was scared to death.

"Can you go put some clothes on, or do you want to go down to the station in that?" Short and Chubby asked.

"Why am I being taken into custody?" I asked, although I already knew what it was about.

They said they needed to question me about a few things. I decided to just go down to the station in what I was wearing, a T-shirt and some pajama pants. I locked my house up and headed to their car. The tall and skinny one opened the back door for me, and then he shut it behind me after I got in. On our way to the Chicago Police Department, I sat in the backseat, wondering if they were going to keep me or if they were really just going to question me.

When we arrived at the station, we went through a secret entrance that I never knew existed. We came to a complete stop in front of a door that read CONVICT ENTRANCE. My heart dropped. Short and Chubby opened the door for me, and I followed them inside. We entered an elevator and headed to the fourth floor. Tall and Skinny headed in a different direction, and Short and Chubby led me into a room. The sign on the door read INTERROGATION.

I sat down on a steel chair. He told me that he'd be back and to just get comfortable. He shut the door, and from the other side I could hear keys jiggling. That let me know that he had locked me in the room. I had seen way too many criminal movies, so I knew that the glass on the wall was a one-way window. They could see me, but I couldn't see them. I remained calm, and I sat there staring at the wall. I didn't want to look guilty, so I aimed for a look of boredom.

When both Short and Tall came back in, I gave them my full attention. Short and Chubby started it off.

"Well, we found your car in the Chicago River, and we've noticed you didn't report it stolen, so—"

"Well, I figured the loan company came and towed it because I was behind on my payments," I quickly lied.

The tall, skinny officer jotted down a few things and looked up at me. "So you know nothing about your car being in the river?" he quizzed.

I shook my head no.

"Well, there was arson activity done to your vehicle *and* DNA from a few people who came up dead. Now, you look pretty harmless, *but* we will be investigating it all. If it comes back that you had anything to do with this"—Short and Chubby stepped closer to my chair—"we will bring you all the way down." He emphasized that point.

I gave him innocent eyes with a slight smile on my face. I didn't want to seem guilty or like I was shitting bricks, because I definitely was. The tall one chuckled and shook his head as they both left the room. Once again they locked the door. I put my head down. It was pounding, and they were making me nervous. After a while, they came back and told me they were taking me home.

When we pulled up to my house, they suggested that I let them know if I found out anything new. They gave me their business cards so that I could contact them. I glanced at Short and Chubby's card, which read DAVID LOBINSKI. I put it in my bra and stepped out of the back of the police car. I ran up my porch steps, unlocked my door, and slammed it behind me.

"What am I going to do?" I asked myself.

I ran upstairs. My legs and hands were shaking. I knew then that I had to leave town. In this day and age, there was too much technology for me *not* to be found responsible for that car incident. I had nothing to do with any dead bodies, and I knew that Chicago was good at framing people for shit, even without any leads.

I was nervous, and I no longer wanted to go out for drinks with Porsha and Kim. Then again, I did need a few drinks. Something told me to go see about that machete on my shelf. When I reached the top of the steps, I ran to my room and grabbed the chair from my vanity. I opened my closet door and placed the chair in the middle of the floor. I stood on top of it. To my surprise, the machete was gone. I slowly looked around the closet, then climbed off the chair and looked around my room cautiously.

I felt like I was in a scary movie and it was my turn to die. I was a nervous wreck. My phone rang, and I almost jumped out of my skin. When I realized it was my phone, I took a deep breath and walked over to my bed to get it. It read PORSHA CALLING. I answered, and she asked for directions to my house. I gave them to her and quickly got dressed.

She blew her horn when she was outside. I didn't feel as cute as I should. I wore a tight yellow dress with some black pumps. I felt like a damn bumblebee, but that was the outcome when you were rushing. Kim was sitting in the front seat of the car. I opened the back door and sat behind Porsha.

Kim turned around and faced me. "Girl, I ain't think you was gon' come," she said, smiling from ear to ear.

I cracked a small smile back. My mind was all over the place. I just kept replaying the whole cop and Josh ordeal in my head. *Somebody is trying to set me up.*

We ended up at Eclipse Restaurant and Lounge on West Diversey. We decided that we would order just appetizers and drinks. I hoped and prayed they wouldn't bring up me getting fired. I should have known better.

Kim had to be the one to investigate the situation further. "So when did you and Cliff start messing around?" she began.

"It was nothing like that," I replied, waving her question off.

Then she insisted that I tell her everything. I refused, and she finally dropped the subject. She went on to ask me about Crystal.

"Do you have any pictures of her?" she asked.

"No. I kind of switched purses, and I didn't put my wallet in this one," I said as I stroked my purse.

She nodded her head and then asked me about my parents, if they were still together.

"No. I wouldn't know my dad if I saw him, and my mom . . . she's okay, I guess," I responded. I started looking around the restaurant because I had the feeling somebody was watching me.

"You okay?" Porsha asked.

I nodded my head yeah and continued sipping my Long Island Iced Tea. They talked in complete circles the entire time we were at the restaurant. I was too busy being worried, trying to figure out who was stalking me, to even care about whatever it was they were talking about.

After we were done with our drinks and food, we decided to head home. They wanted to set up another date and figured we should all do something every Friday. I didn't like the whole idea, but I went along with the flow.

When we got to my block, there were police cars all over the place. They both looked back at me as we slowly drove down my street.

"They're at your door," Kim said. I looked out my window and saw that the police were indeed at my door.

"Take me to my mom's. I know they want to question me about my neighbor whose husband whupped her ass earlier. I don't have anything to do with that," I said, lying. I sat back. I was so scared, and I couldn't allow them see me sweat.

They both laughed.

"I know what you mean." Porsha laughed.

Their giggling made me feel better. I sat in the backseat, wondering why the police had returned. They must've come back to arrest me, since there were so many of them.

I just prayed that my mom was home.

Chapter 11

I told Porsha and Kim that they didn't have to wait for me to get in the house, because my mom was always there. I knew that was far from the truth. I hadn't been to see my mom in years, and I really didn't see the point in being here. She had made it clear that she couldn't stand me.

I knocked on the door firmly. I could hear her getting up to answer the door. She looked through the curtain that covered the window on the door. She opened the door. If looks could kill, I would have been dead from her mean mug.

She didn't say a word. She just moved out of the way so that I could enter. I looked at her small frame and knew that she wasn't doing well. The house looked no different from how it had looked when I lived here.

I sat down on the couch and watched my mother as she sat down on the other end of it. She stared at me with so much hatred in her eyes. I just shook my head.

"What brings you?" she asked, knowing there had to be a reason.

"Just wanted to see you," I lied.

She let out a small laugh and then said, "You know you're wanted, right?" She already knew I was aware of it.

I let out a sigh. "How you know?"

"You're only on the news. You ain't been taking them meds, have you?"

I just rolled my eyes. She knew how I felt about those pills. I told her that I poured them down the toilet. She shook her head as she stood up and went to go get something.

Cancer had made my mother lose all her hair and a lot of weight. She looked sickly, and I could tell that this disease was eating her alive. She had gotten cancer from smoking cigarettes on a daily basis. She was one of those people that said she would never get cancer, yet she was taken by storm.

She came back with my diploma from my behavioral high school and took her seat at the end of the couch. I looked at it, and a tear fell. ANGEL CRYSTAL JACOBS, CLASS OF 2003. I looked at it and then back at my mom.

"You know that was the happiest day of my life. And even though I may have acted as if I hated you"—she shook her head as tears rolled down her face—"I didn't and I don't. I was just so hurt, Crystal. So hurt."

I scooted down to her and grabbed her, and we embraced. This was the first time we had hugged each other in over two decades.

She looked me in the eyes and said, "I'm sorry for everything he did to you. I know you must hate me for allowing it, but, baby, I was dumb." She cried. I just held her. I didn't know what she was talking about. She had even called me by my sister's name, so I figured she had the two of us mixed up.

The news had come on, and my mother turned it up.

"Chicago breaking news . . . Officials think they have discovered who the Chicago serial killer is. They say it's a woman by the name of Angel Jacobs. Officials say they believe she tried to dispose of her car so that she couldn't be traced. They found a pair of her red leather gloves that had DNA from Mitchell Perry and another man. Police are on a manhunt, trying to find Miss Jacobs. We have footage of her in a convenience store, buying lighter fluid," said the blue-eyed reporter.

They showed the video of me at the store, buying the lighter fluid. My heart dropped. Something had told me to put that shit down, but I had ignored it. Then Josh was talking to the reporter.

"Here's one of the lucky victims who she didn't finish off correctly," the male reporter said with a microphone in his hand.

Josh stood there, nodding his head.

"So tell us, Joshua, what exactly happened that night?" the reporter asked.

"I took her to a hotel with me, and she tried to choke me to death. I saw her in the store the day she bought the lighter fluid and knew she must have killed someone else," he said, breathing heavily.

"She's known to be dangerous and malicious," the reporter said, ending the conversation. Then the subject changed to the weather.

My body started shaking, and my mother looked at me and said, "You need to either turn yourself in or leave town." She started breathing weird, and then she collapsed. I rushed over to her and began shaking her.

"Ma! Ma! Wake up, please!" I begged. I was just now getting closer to my mother, and here she was, lying on the floor. I cried and screamed. I didn't want to call the police, but I had to. I told them where to come. I checked my mother's pulse. She was gone.

I kissed her on the forehead, and then I left. I took the back roads so that I could use a pay phone. I called Omar, and he answered on the first ring.

"Omar, I need you!" I cried.

"Angel?"

"Yes! Please come and get me," I begged. I kept looking around, hoping nobody saw me. I told him where I was, and he said he'd be there in fifteen minutes. It suddenly started pouring. I stayed in the phone booth and waited for Omar.

A while later his Charger pulled up. I ran and got in.

"Baby, you're all over the news," he told me as he pulled off.

I started crying as I held my face in my hands. I didn't know what to say. I was a wanted woman, and I had just lost my mother.

"It's gon' be cool, baby," Omar assured me while he rubbed my back.

I was torn and had no place to go. I couldn't go to jail. My sister needed me. We pulled up to a run-down house on the east side of Chicago. I didn't complain, but I would never allow myself to stay at a dope house. At this point in time, I was desperate. We ran up to the porch as the rain continued to pour down.

He unlocked the door and led me in. The inside of the house shocked me. It was the complete opposite of the outside. It was well decorated, and it screamed "Expensive!" Omar was at the door, taking all his clothes off, and I just slipped out of my shoes.

"Sit down," he demanded.

I went to take a seat on the cream sofa. I knew he wanted me to explain what was going on. I didn't know myself. When he was stripped down to his boxers and socks, he came and sat down next to me.

"Now, what's going on?" He was puzzled.

"Baby," I said, shaking my head, "I honestly don't know!" I put my hand on his leg and said, "I think somebody is trying to set me up." I wasn't lying. I wasn't capable of killing anybody.

He looked into my eyes and shook his head. He grabbed me and held me tight. I could feel the love that he had for me through his touch. "You gotta leave town," he whispered.

I agreed, and I already knew that my only outlet was Cliff. We watched the news again, and it seemed as if I was on every other channel. My name was tied to several murders, and they were saying that I was the worst killer yet. They were warning all men to stay clear of me. There was a cash reward for any leads that led to my arrest.

I was praying that all of this was all just a bad dream, and that when I woke up in the morning, things would be back to normal. I knew they wouldn't, though. I just couldn't understand who would want to send me away for the rest of my life. I felt the world closing in on me.

Omar turned the TV off and carried me upstairs. He set me on his king-sized, wood-framed bed and kissed me on the forehead. He kept asking me to tell him about myself, but I couldn't. It wasn't that I didn't want to tell him; I just couldn't remember anything.

He held me close to him throughout the night. Before I fell asleep, he whispered in my ear, "I love you." I smiled. Through all the pain and the losses I had endured, I managed to smile. I wished that I could clear my slate and be with him, but it was impossible. He was too young, and clearly, my life was coming to an end.

Although I was in a fucked-up situation, him telling me that he loved me made me want to fuck him. I began kissing his muscular, tatted-up chest, and he started rubbing my ass. I pulled his dick out of his boxers and began sucking on it.

While giving him head, I replayed the last conversation I had with my mom. I was sad that she had died, but I wasn't hurt, because we never had that bond. I felt like she must have known that she was getting ready to die, because she wanted closure with me. It was fucked up that she didn't even mention Crystal. I had to get in touch with Tiffany to let her know I had to leave town and I wasn't going to be able to take Crystal with me.

I continued sucking Omar's dick to perfection, and then I started spelling my name in cursive with my tongue on his shaft. He lifted my head and started kissing me on my lips. He put his dick in my pussy and started grinding in me. He kissed my neck and flicked his finger across my clit. I was on cloud nine. At that very moment, I forgot about all the trouble that I was in.

He worked me slowly. He lifted my legs up on his shoulders so that he could get deeper inside of me. The deeper he went, the louder I moaned. He started slapping my ass, and I loved every bit of it.

"I'm about to cum," he whispered to me. I didn't recall him putting a condom on, and I figured he was telling me this because he hadn't. I didn't care, though. He loved me, and I loved him too.

"Cum, baby," I moaned.

He pushed himself deeper in me and stopped moving. His body went limp as sweat dripped from both of our foreheads. I wiped his forehead off with my hand as he lay on top of me and told me that he loved me again. We lay there, naked, and eventually we fell asleep.

When I woke up, Omar was nowhere in sight. I slipped back into my clothes and searched the house. I found a cordless phone sitting on the receiver in his kitchen. I decided to check my voice mail. I had a few messages from Kim and Porsha, one from Cliff, and one from Omar. I listened to the one from Omar several times as tears fell from my eyes.

"Baby, I love you a lot, and I know you got yourself in some shit. In the room there's an envelope with some thousands in it. You gotta leave town, and that should help you for a while. I don't want to let you go, but I understand I have to. Be safe and be good. Love you."

I had finally found somebody who cared about me, and I had to leave him. I had only one place to run to. A place where I knew I would be taken care of, and that was with Cliff. I called him, and he answered happily. I told him that I had decided to move with him. He was happy, and he told me that he could have me on the next plane, which would depart in three hours. That was fine with me, so after we hung up, I went upstairs and searched the room for the envelope Omar had left me.

I found it under the pillow that I had been lying on. The envelope had five thousand dollars in it. I cried after counting it. I had never had that much money at once. He loved me enough to aid me in my escape from Chicago.

I needed to change my identity. There was no way I would catch a cab to the airport without a disguise. I went in the bathroom and stood in front of the mirror. I started braiding my hair straight back. When I was done with that, I went in Omar's closet and put on one of his sweat suits. I looked like a stud, but that was the look I was aiming for. I sprayed some of his Gucci cologne on my neck and decided that that was the icing on the cake. I then called a cab to meet me around the corner.

I decided to write Omar a note before I departed. I found an envelope and a pen. I turned the envelope the long way and began to pour out my heart.

> *Omar,*
> *I never would have imagined that I would have these feelings for you. I really do love you, and I hate the fact that I have to leave, but if it's meant to be, we'll be. Can't wait until I see you again. Love you forever and always.*

I kissed the envelope and held it close to my chest. I wished we had spent more time together, but it was a little too late. I put the envelope on his bed and went downstairs to leave. I turned the lock on the inside of the doorknob and shut the door.

There was no turning back.

My journey officially began once I got outside to the cab. The cabdriver was already there, waiting for me. It appeared to the cabdriver that I had come from the back of my house. I had actually come from the alley. I got in the cab and directed the Arabian driver to take me to the airport.

Chapter 12

When I reached the airport in Atlanta, Cliff and his bodyguard were sitting in the lobby, waiting on me. I was still dressed in my stud attire, so the facial expressions they were making weren't shocking to me at all. Many people approached Cliff for pictures and autographs, but he politely turned them down.

When I got within his arms' reach, he embraced me. I didn't hug him back. I just smiled a fake smile. He looked at me sideways and he grabbed my hand as we started walking.

"Why do you have that shit on?" His voice was deep and low. I just shrugged my shoulders. I didn't feel like getting into all the details as to why I had this *shit* on. I was caught up in my thoughts about my sister and the death of my mother.

When we walked outside, the sun was scorching. With the sweat suit I had on, I was damn near dead. We all climbed into a black Suburban and pulled off. I fell asleep during the drive to wherever we were going. I hadn't got the opportunity to sleep on the plane, because I didn't want anyone at any moment to recognize me. Hours later we pulled up to his estate. He woke me up.

"Go straight upstairs and change up out of that shit. I bought you a few outfits. They're lying on the bed," he said, climbing out of the car. I got out and followed his instructions.

Inside, there were so many niggas hanging around that I felt uncomfortable. I rushed past the four that were blocking the stairway. I ran up the steps, not really sure which room he was referring to. I went in at least three rooms before I discovered the room with my clothes. I looked over the outfits, and they all were True Religion. There were heels for every outfit, and they all were designed by Christian Louboutin.

As I was looking over the attire, Cliff walked in with a Victoria's Secret bag.

"Here's some underwear and body lotion," he said, handing the bag to me. "I wasn't sure what smell you liked, so I got the one I liked." He chuckled.

I smiled as I grabbed the bag and pulled the body lotion out. It was Pure Seduction, my second favorite scent, so it was okay.

He told me I could shower in the bathroom adjoining the room I was in. "If you need anything, don't hesitate to ask, because I'd be happy to get it for you."

Finally, I felt like he was the Cliff that I had first met. I was enjoying every minute of it. I gathered the things I wanted to wear that day and headed to the bathroom. As I scrubbed my skin clean, I had a flashback of me waving bye to Crystal as she got in the car with Tiffany. I also replayed my mom telling me to leave town and Omar holding me tight through the night. I slid down the shower wall and cried my eyes out.

When I finally got myself together, I turned the water off and dried off. I slipped into the black lace boy short panties, hooked the matching bra, and then I put my new Pure Seduction lotion all over my body. I put on the True Religion jean vest and shorts and sprayed myself with the matching mist. I walked out of the bathroom with the clothes I had on earlier balled up in my hands.

Cliff grabbed them from me. "You don't mind if I throw these away, do you?" He smiled.

I did mind, because they were the only thing I had left of Omar. I didn't want to start a fuss, so I shook my head no, and he walked away with the clothes. I watched him leave the room.

I sat down on the bed and sighed. I needed a breakthrough. I knew it wouldn't be long before the news about the murders hit the national TV stations, and I didn't want to be here when it did.

Cliff came back into the room and sat down next to me. "I don't want you to be bored. I'm gonna have my little sister, Chelsea, come and keep you company. She'll be in town within an hour or so." He rubbed my hair.

"Thanks," I said. I didn't know if I was supposed to be thankful or not.

He told me that he would be going out of town for a fight next week and that if I wanted to come, I could. I really didn't want to be in the public eye, so I told him I'd think about it.

"I'm about to head to the store. You want anything?" he asked before he left the room.

I told him no. I pulled the covers back on the bed and got under them. I was exhausted, and my body needed to rest.

Later I went downstairs and Cliff was nowhere in sight. There was a guy sitting on the couch, watching TV, in a room that had a pool table, arcade games, a bar, and a stripper pole. He couldn't see me, because I could see only the back of his head.

I walked in front of the TV. He had to be the finest man I had ever seen. He resembled Cliff and had dreads just like him. He had a caramel skin complexion and brown eyes, with a scar under his right eye. He was muscular and had tats on his chest and all over his arms. The fact that he was shirtless took my mind elsewhere.

"Um, you kn-n-now where Cliff is?" I stuttered. I wasn't expecting to come across anybody that looked this good.

"He went to gamble," he said, not really paying me any attention. I didn't know if it was the way he looked or the fact that he wasn't paying attention to me that made me want him.

"Know when he'll be back?" I asked as I took a seat on the same couch he sat on.

He shook his head no and continued watching the movie *Life*. I sat there a little while longer, fantasizing about all the things I would do to him if I got the chance. I would suck the skin off of his dick and make his toes curl. He was just that sexy. I watched him as he sipped his Gatorade and licked his lips. He knew exactly what he was doing, teasing me.

"So you Angel?" he asked, still never looking my way.

"Yeah. And you are?" I was anxious to know.

"Tristan. I'm Cliff's little brother." He finally looked my way, and I must say, that scar made him look so thuggish.

"Oh, really? How old are you?" I asked, trying to make it seem as if I wanted to know their age difference.

"I'm twenty-four. We four years apart," he said with a Southern accent. He was right up my alley. He was two years younger than me, but I had discovered that the younger niggas were better lovers. I wondered how loyal he was to Cliff and if he would consider fucking me.

We heard somebody coming into the room, and we both looked back. It was Cliff and his bodyguard.

"I'm glad you two met," Cliff said as he grabbed my arm for me to stand up. I stood up, and he wrapped his arm around me. "This is my little brother, Trist, and this my ole lady, Angel."

I smiled. I did not want to be known as his woman.

Tristan cracked a small smile and nodded his head, as if to say "What up?" and then directed his attention to the movie.

Cliff grabbed my arm and escorted me out of the room and up the stairs to the master bedroom. He closed the door behind us and gave me this look that told me he was upset.

"Don't let me catch you back in there," he said firmly.

"Why?" I questioned. I didn't see what the problem was. He walked up on me and back-handed the spit out of my mouth. I flipped onto the bed and held my face. I looked up at him with my eyes filled with tears.

He pointed his finger at me and yelled, "Don't ever question me! *Ever!*"

My face was stinging badly. The pain was sharp, and I knew he hadn't changed, because no one changed overnight. I had just never expected to get this treatment so soon. As I lay on the bed, I cried and cried. I needed to escape from Cliff.

An hour passed, and in walked a thick, light-skinned girl. She had on the tightest leggings, which complemented her nice frame. She was very pretty and had a long black weave that hung down her back. I sat up, still holding my cheek with my hand.

"You okay?" she asked. She shut the door behind her. She sat down on the bed with me. I still had my hand over my left cheek. She slowly pulled my hand from it. Her expression let me know that the wound, which I hadn't seen yet, didn't look too good. "Yeah, he left a mark. You need to put something on it."

She went to the bathroom and came back with a cold rag. She placed it on my cheek. I held it there, and she sat there watching me, shaking her head. "You gotta be careful with Cliff. He got some serious anger problems," she said. "I'm Chelsea, his little sister. You must be Angel."

She stared at me as I nodded my head.

She put her hand on my head and laughed. "We got to get rid of these jail braids, Mama." She chuckled. I had forgotten that I even had them in my hair.

"You're right," I confessed. No wonder Trist had barely looked my way. I looked like a Hebrew slave fresh off the slave ship.

She left the room and came back with a comb. "Sit on the floor," she said.

I slid off the bed and onto the floor. Chelsea started taking my braids down. After that, she washed my hair for me.

"You wear a weave?" she asked.

I told her that I had never had any in my hair. She brought a bag full of hair equipment and started doing my hair. When she was done, I had an invisible part with a long sew-in. I ran to look in the mirror that was attached to the dresser. I loved the way it hung on my back. I ran my fingers through the long black weave and smiled.

"I like it," I said as I turned around and gave her a hug.

"Good. Now, let me arch your eyebrows and put you on some lashes." She was smiling from ear to ear, and I was eager to see how they would turn out.

After the lashes and eyebrows were done, I went back to look in the mirror. I loved the way I looked. For the first time in a long time, I actually thought that I looked beautiful.

Chelsea sat on the bed. "Do you want to ride with me to my doctor's appointment?"

"Sure," I responded while she looked over at the heels that were on the floor and picked up the red ones.

"Hun, put these on," she suggested, handing them to me. She gave me some gold accessories, and I put those on too. She looked me over and smiled. She was having fun dressing me up, obviously. "You look like a model."

"Do I?" I asked.

She grabbed my hand and looked at my nails. "Well you did until I noticed your nails weren't done. We have to do something about this after my appointment," she insisted. She let go of my hand, and I looked at my nails. They didn't look that bad.

We both headed downstairs and out the door. Chelsea was driving an all-black Bentley coupe. It was evident that she had money. I just wondered if it was from her brother or if she had made it on her own.

"What you do for a living?" I asked.

"Well, I'm a stripper, I do music videos, and I host events," she said, starting her car up and driving off.

"Really? You make good money doing that?" I was curious. I had thought about stripping when I lost my job at the law firm. I never knew strippers lived like this.

"Yeah, real good money," she said. She began telling me that she worked at various strip clubs in different states. She was loved mostly at Magic City in Atlanta and King of Diamonds, otherwise known as KOD, in Miami.

The doctor's office that we pulled up to was called Swan Center.

"I come here to get my butt injections. I'm also going to come here to get my breast implants done," Chelsea revealed. She also slid in there that if I wanted anything done, she knew her brother wouldn't mind paying for it.

When we got out of her Bentley, I walked behind her and admired her ass. It did sit nice, and it also looked very real. I thought it wouldn't hurt to find out more about the procedure.

I could tell that Chelsea was well known in this office, because everyone was talking to her about everything except her appointment. We patiently sat in the waiting room. My phone began to vibrate. It was Cliff.

When I answered, he was very apologetic about the situation that had happened earlier. I accepted his apology, although I knew he was capable of doing it again. I told him that I was with Chelsea at her doctor's appointment. He volunteered that if I wanted anything done, I knew where to get the money from. It was something to consider.

While Chelsea kept Angel occupied and out of Tristan's view, Cliff decided this was a great opportunity to call Porsha. Porsha was shocked to learn that Angel was in Atlanta. They had been together just the day before. She told Cliff that she thought that Angel was wanted for murder. Cliff was thrown by this news because Angel looked harmless and never tried anything whenever he put his hands on her.

"Albert does not want the police to get her. Is there any way you can change her identity or anything?" Porsha asked desperately.

Cliff thought for a little while and then said, "I mean, maybe some plastic surgery."

Porsha was relieved. Albert had warned her that if he couldn't get his hands on Angel because of her stupidity, then she was as good as gone too. Porsha could not let her chance of being married and having a man slip through her fingers because of Angel's selfish ass.

Although Cliff was filthy rich, he wanted that money. He already had plans for it. He would love to see Angel in a new way. He was tired of that little-ass wrap and those plain-ass clothes.

"When is he getting out?" Cliff wondered aloud. The last time he had spoken to Porsha, she'd told him Albert would be released in a month or so. That was three months ago.

"He told me a few months. He won't tell me the exact date," she said.

Cliff shook his head. Porsha was a dumb broad. "Okay, I'll call you to let you know if Angel agrees to the procedure."

Porsha promised him that Albert would pay him for the little bit of nothing that he was doing. They said their good-byes and ended the call.

Cliff decided to send Angel a text telling her that he would love her to get a little more junk in her trunk. He also suggested some face surgery, maybe on her nose or lips. He thought she'd be upset, but to his surprise, she agreed.

He put his phone on the bed and lay down on his back. He lay there pondering whether he should even allow Angel to hang around Chelsea's slutty ass or Trist. He knew she was good for introducing his girlfriends to the fast life, and Tristan was simply good for turning them out.

Chapter 13

I had just gotten my plastic surgery the day before, and now I was lying in the bed, unable to move. Cliff and Chelsea had insisted on butt injections. Even though I had really wanted only a lip and a nose job, I'd decided to get the butt injections too. I loved the way I looked but was tired of having to watch my back. I needed some type of disguise that would allow me to walk the streets of Atlanta freely. Plus, Cliff was the one paying for everything.

Chelsea and I had become close over the few weeks that she was here. She told me that she didn't care about who or what I did, because her brother was an abusive male ho. I totally agreed. I couldn't wait until the swelling went down, because I was ready to see who the new me could attract.

Cliff was in and out of town, and I was so grateful for every departure. He was really smothering me. Ever since Chelsea had given me a makeover, he wanted me to be in his sight at all times. It was very annoying, and I just knew that after I bounced back from the surgery, he would be even further down my throat.

Chelsea came into my room with some girl that looked like a stripper. I sat up so that I could face them as they took a seat on the bed.

"Angel, this my girl Beautyful," Chelsea said, introducing the Asian and black mixed girl. She had long black hair and a body that I assumed was made. She was shaped like an hourglass.

I said, "Hi."

Then Chelsea started up. "What you think about going to Miami with us in a few weeks?" she asked.

I didn't know why she'd asked me that. I was appalled. I didn't know what to say. "Why?" I asked. I had never traveled before. All I knew was Chicago, and now Atlanta. I really didn't mind going to Miami, but I figured they were going there only to strip.

"Well, we're working, but we're also hosting a few parties," Beautyful answered. She was very pretty. She appeared to be flawless, well, at least to me.

"Yeah, and that week Cliff is gon' be in Las Vegas, so you'll be bored and home alone here," Chelsea added.

I wasn't sure if Cliff would even allow me to go. He was controlling, and I wasn't down for a beat down over a Miami trip.

"Don't worry about Cliff. I'll just tell him we're going to Charlotte to visit my granny," Chelsea assured me. She told me that he never questioned her. "Trust me," she said.

I agreed to go, and they both got up and headed out the door.

"Oh yeah, we'll be picking out your gear," Chelsea added before closing the door behind her.

I put my head back down on the pillow. *Why is everybody targeting the way I dress?* I stared at the ceiling and imagined what Miami would be like. They said it was Urban Beach Week, so there would be hella niggas. I was ready.

The swelling from my surgery had gone down, and I was feeling beautiful. I barely recognized myself. I stood in the full-body mirror and admired the new me. I was a flawless beauty.

Cliff walked up behind me and wrapped his arms around me. "You look good, baby," he said while kissing the back of my neck.

I continued admiring myself, and then I headed downstairs to show Trist. When I almost reached the bottom of the staircase, he came through the door. He hadn't seen me since the day I had come back from the procedure. He was staring hard, not paying attention to what he was doing. He watched me like a hawk, licked his lips, and bumped right into Cliff.

"You wanna pay attention to what you doing?" Cliff said sarcastically.

I stood at the bottom of the steps, looking dumbfounded. I had been too busy watching Trist my damn self that I hadn't noticed that Cliff was present. Cliff started to go up the stairs, and then he stopped when he reached me.

"Keep trying me, Angel," he warned. I stood there speechless. He continued up the steps, and I continued going down them.

I walked into the living room to find Trist sitting on the couch with his feet up on the coffee table. I didn't know what it was, but it seemed like I wasn't supposed to be around him. That was the vibe Cliff was giving me, besides the fact that Trist was his brother and I shouldn't be all up in his face, anyway.

He looked in my direction. "What's up?" he said.

I shook my head and headed into the kitchen. I knew that I had gone downstairs to get his attention. After that little warning from Cliff, I had changed my mind.

I sat at the gray-and-black decorated glass table and stared out the curtainless window. I wondered what Crystal was doing, because I hadn't talked to her in a few weeks. I had tried calling her, but Tiffany's phone was off. I hoped she didn't think I had forgotten about her, because that definitely was not an option.

"What you thinking about?" I turned around and saw Trist rummaging in the refrigerator.

I turned back around and said, "Just day-dreaming." I wanted to get up and go in another room, but I didn't want to appear to be running from him.

"I know you scared of my brother and all," he said as he walked closer. "I also know you want me." He was confident.

I smiled, because he was absolutely right. I was glad my back was facing him so that he couldn't see me blushing.

"If that's the case, it's cool, because I want you too. And if you know anything about me, then you'll know I get what I want," he told me. I heard him shut the refrigerator door. As he started walking toward the kitchen door, he added, "In due time, baby. In due time."

I was happy we were on the same page. I hadn't had sex since Omar, and I was fiending. I was happy that Cliff wasn't trying to fuck me, being that I was sore. I knew that he would try to get some soon, and I just prayed it wouldn't be today.

Cliff came into the kitchen shortly after Trist left. I was scared straight. I thought he had heard everything that Trist had just said to me. It was obvious that I kept getting in trouble for all the things Trist was doing.

"Baby, there's a ceremony tonight, and you're coming with me. Chelsea gon' help you find something to wear, so get up and get ready," he instructed.

I got up from the table and did as I was told. Finally, I had my own closet. It was a huge walk-in closet that was nowhere near filled. I had only about twenty outfits, but being that I had a whole new shape and size, I figured I couldn't fit into any of it, anyway. I pulled out a pair of jeggings, the new leggings that looked like blue jeans, from my drawer and threw on a white wife beater. I grabbed my red Christian Louboutin heels and my red Louis Vuitton handbag from my accessory section. I wore a long gold necklace, three gold bangles, and some big golden hoops. I sprayed my Gucci Guilty perfume and headed out.

Cliff, bombarded me, preventing me from leaving. "You think that's appropriate?" he questioned, looking me up and down.

I looked down at the floor and shrugged my shoulders.

"Baby, listen," he said as he grabbed my face gently, "I don't want no nigga hounding you. You mine, and I want the world to know that."

"I know you don't mean no harm," I said, lying through my teeth. All he meant was harm when it came to me.

He kissed me on my forehead, and it reminded me of Omar. Then he released my face. "You need a new name, too," he stated. "So what's it gon' be?"

"Crystal," I said without thinking twice. I headed out of the room with a whole new attitude. I would be Crystal from now on, and I was, in fact, a bad bitch. Soon Atlanta would know that.

Chelsea and Beautyful stood at the bottom of the stairs with big smiles on their faces.

"Look at that goddess!" Beautyful said.

Chelsea nodded her head in agreement.

They just didn't know how much all of this was blowing my head up. "Yes, look at me now." I giggled.

"Angel, you gon' kill 'em," Chelsea joked.

I laughed because she was right. "By the way, the name is Crystal," I told them.

"Oh my, the girl is brand new!" Chelsea said as she slapped Beautyful's hand.

We went out the door. None of us saw Cliff at the top of the steps, angry as ever. Nor did we see Trist at the living room door, admiring me. I guess we were caught up in the moment.

We rode to Lennox Mall in Beautyful's BMW. These girls were crafted at what they did, because they were riding and living well. I was in the backseat, sightseeing. I had never been anywhere without Cliff, except to Chelsea's doctor's appointment.

When we got to the mall, men and women had their eyes on us. In my opinion, the females were staring harder than the men. A group of guys who looked like they had long money approached us.

"What's up, Beautyful and Luxury?" said the dark-skinned guy with the gold grill in his mouth.

"Hey, baby," Chelsea answered. They both gave him a hug. I figured Luxury was Chelsea's stripping name. I stood there, silent, as I felt the other guys' eyes on my ass.

"Y'all work tonight?" A light-skinned, sexy guy asked them. His diamonds sparkled the entire time we were in his presence.

They both said no, and then Beautyful told them we had to get going. Once we walked into the first store that caught our interest, the shopping began. In there, they told me that they got niggas approaching them all the time, thinking they knew them. They said they didn't mind it, though. I wanted to know what exactly had made them want to start stripping.

"Just something to do," Beautyful said and giggled.

"We just started doing it, and then we got fame from it. People started asking us to do videos, and then that turned into fucking celebrities and getting jobs hosting at various events. Now we paid!" Chelsea added, giving me the rundown.

I listened, soaking up every piece of information given to me.

"Yeah, Cliff will take good care of you, but what's better than having ya own? At any given time, a nigga can just throw you out, 'cause he know you'll need him. You gotta get your own, just in case," Beautyful told me.

She was making a lot of sense. I thought about the five stacks Omar had given me. I decided I would use that as rainy day money. I would soon find out, though, that the lifestyle I was being introduced to would make that five thousand dollars look like lunch money.

The light-skinned guy that was with the group of niggas came in the store and walked up to me. "What's yo' name?" he asked.

I wondered what made him come to *me*. "Crystal," I said confidently.

"I'm Jeremy. Put my number in yo' phone," he demanded.

I pulled my phone out of my bag and entered his number and name. He told me I looked foreign and that he liked my proper voice. I told him I would call him, and then he left the store.

I had all intentions of calling him. He was sexy, and he was the only attractive one in the group. He didn't know me, and neither did anyone else in this city, so I could fuck and suck whomever I wanted.

Even thought my appearance had changed, my appetite for sex surely hadn't. If anything, it had gotten bigger. The thought of no one knowing me made me just want to have one-night stands with any and everybody.

"He has money. He tips real good at Magic City," Chelsea informed me. I looked at her with uncertainty. "Don't worry. I won't tell Cliff. Truth be told, he don't deserve you, so do you, Mama," she said as she showed me a cream leather jacket and some straight-legged jeans with cutout holes in them.

The outfit, shoes, and accessories came out to a little over three thousand dollars. It looked pretty plain to me. They both found it cute and decided to get the same thing in different colors.

"I think Cliff ain't gon' feel this outfit," I told them. I grew nervous.

"Oh, that ain't for the ceremony. That's for afterward, when we go for drinks *without* Cliff," said Chelsea as she led us into another store to find me a dress.

The Ceremony was held at the Velvet Room, a nightclub. They had shut it down and were using it as the venue for this particular event. The whole club was red. I thought it was cute since Cliff and I were both wearing red.

We looked like the happiest couple alive, taking numerous photos on the red carpet, kissing and hugging all over every other minute. He was being so kind and loving to me, and I saw why I had developed a few feelings for him in the beginning. Everyone complimented him on me. A few of his friends were even checking me out. He told me not to speak unless I was spoken to, so I was quiet for the most part. In other words, I was his trophy.

The food was catered, and there were way too many drinks flowing among the people. Cliff was drunk before long, and every word that came out of his mouth was slurred. His bodyguard had to practically carry him out when it was over.

After the ceremony, we headed to our limo to go home. Cliff's drunk ass was in my ear the entire time, telling me how good he was going to fuck me. I was hoping like hell he would go home and fall asleep, but he was too persistent.

When we got home, we went straight to our bedroom. I peeled my dress off and laid it on the bed. He started kissing me on the neck and telling me how bad he wanted to taste me. I really wasn't in the mood to fuck him. I also knew better then to deny him.

He slid my red thong off and began drinking my juices. I was feeling too good to tell him to stop, and after a while I didn't want him to. I was on cloud nine. When he lifted his head up, I saw Mike. I started screaming at the top of my lungs. I grabbed his face, and he grabbed my hands and pinned them down. He started to kiss me sloppily on the mouth. I was disgusted and wanted him off of me so bad. The more I resisted, the more he wanted from me.

He stuck his dick in without putting on a condom. He started stroking me fast and rough. My inner thigh was in pain, and my pussy was sore. I kept saying "Ow!" but that didn't make the situation any better. He put his hand over my mouth. He pinned my legs so far back that I thought they would break. He continued to hump me fast and hard. I prayed he would cum sooner rather than later.

After ten minutes of pure pain, he came. His body lay heavy on mine, and he was breathing like a monster. He repeatedly told me he loved me, and then he was sound asleep. I slid from under him and went to take a shower.

I had plans.

Chapter 14

We ended up at Club Edge on Edgewater Avenue. We went straight to the VIP line, and this dark-skinned nigga paid for us all to get in. When we got inside the club, he guided us to his VIP table, where there was plenty of Cîroc and Hennessy for the entire club.

We sat down and got acquainted with all the other niggas that were in the VIP section. The nigga who paid our way sat down next to me. I was rocking all black, and my tight dress complemented my new curves. The music was loud, so I could barely hear what he was saying.

When he leaned in closer and repeated what he said the first time, I heard him say, "Let me pay for it." He was referring to my ass.

"It's not for sale," I replied.

He looked at me and smiled. He got up and headed elsewhere.

"What did he say?" Beautyful asked.

I told her what he said, and she looked at me
like I was stupid. She gave me that "Why didn't
you take the offer?" face. I began to realize that
if the price was right, anything went with these
two. I loved sex dearly. The thing was, I hadn't
had any good sex in a while. It wasn't like the guy
knew me or would ever see me again. I started
to regret that I didn't take him up on the offer.
I would have gotten two of my favorite things
from him: sex *and* money

A few niggas came and sat in between the
three of us. A nigga was in both Chelsea's and
Beautyful's ears. The one sitting next to me was
about to get in my ear until Mr. Pay Our Way
came and dismissed him.

He got back in my ear and said, "Yeah, I'm
persistent."

We both shared a laugh. I had made up my
mind that I would fuck him. I did have sex with
Cliff all of three hours ago, but I hadn't wanted it
or enjoyed that. I decided that I would make up
for the loss.

We all decided that we would leave the club
early. We followed him and his boys in Beautyful's BMW. We ended up at the Hyatt Regency,
where we got three separate rooms. While they
got the rooms in order, the girls schooled me.

"Get your money up front. Don't let that nigga
hit you with the okeydoke," Chelsea warned.

"Nothing less than a stack," Beautyful added.

"Oh yeah, and no sucking dick. You don't know him like that," Chelsea mentioned.

I stood there nodding my head. I was soaking all the information in. It was crazy that not that long ago I was in Chicago, with a professional job, and now I was on the run in Atlanta, being a ho.

They signaled for us to hurry up as we all headed to the elevator. While in it, Mr. Pay Our Way put his hands up my skirt. He was playing with my pussy, which was still a little tender from Cliff. He was licking on my earlobe and talking dirty in my ear.

When the elevator reached the sixth floor, we all got off and followed the guys to the designated rooms. As soon as Mr. Pay Our Way and I got into our room, he turned the lights out. I quickly turned them back on.

"As much as I wanna fuck you, I'm gon' need mine now," I said with my hand out. He dug in his pocket and peeled off twenty-one hundred-dollar bills. He put the rest of his money in his smoke-gray Crown Holder jeans and recounted the bills meant for me.

After he was sure it was the correct amount, he handed the money to me. I put the money in my handbag and set it on the table. He hit the light switch again and pushed me down on the bed.

He bit my black G-string off and began nibbling on my clit. I instantly got wet. He slurped on my juices, and then he came up and started kissing his way up my neck. I could barely see him in the dark. All I could see was his silhouette. He put on a condom and slid his thick dick inside. He rolled his hips, which made his dick twirl inside my pussy. I held on to his shoulders firmly.

He then started thrusting his body against mine quickly. It was like he was in a rush. I went along with the flow as I tried to hump him back. Then he slowed down his pace, and all I could hear were my juices making a gushy noise.

He whispered something in my ear, but all I heard was, "You'll never see our daughter." I knew I didn't have anything handy to hit him with. I couldn't see his face, but I knew it was Mike's trifling ass. He was fucking me in a rough way now, and I knew he was just trying to be funny.

I couldn't wait until he got up off of me, because I knew I would handle his ass. We fucked all of five minutes before his no-stamina ass came. He got up off of me, rolled over, and fell asleep within minutes. He was snoring loudly, and that let me know he was in a deep sleep. I put a pillow over his head and sat on it. He woke up and began kicking and moving his arms franticly.

"Mike, now who ain't gon' see her?" I asked.

With all the hollering he was doing, I didn't hear a response. When his body no longer moved, I hopped up off his head. I took the pillow from off his head and went back to those stacks in his pockets, which would take an entire day to count. I stuffed them in my bag and got dressed.

"I wonder if a dead man's dick can get hard," I said as I made my way back over to him to see if it could. I put his dick in my mouth, and I sucked on it for a minute. It still was soft and flimsy. I got angry. I looked in my bag for anything to harm him with, but all I could find was an eyebrow archer. I took the top off and sliced his dick up.

"You trifling bitch! You didn't have any problems getting your dick hard when we made our daughter!" I screamed. I continued slicing his dick until he was lying in his own puddle of blood on the bed. "Where is she, Mike? Where is she?" I cried.

I longed to see my daughter, and I knew she felt the same. I got up and went to the window and threw the archer out of it. I got in the other bed, and I lay still. I cried, thinking about my child. Mike was an evil-ass bastard for keeping us from each other. There was no way he could care for her better than I could. Now that he was dead, they would grant me custody. There were knocks on the door, and I grabbed my bag and crept to the door. I looked through the peephole, and standing on the other side of the door were Chelsea and Beautyful. I opened the door halfway.

"Bitch, come on! We hit a lick," Chelsea whispered.

I stepped into the hallway and shut the door behind me, and we ran to the elevator. When we reached the main floor, we ran out to the car. It felt like a weight had been lifted off my shoulders. We sped all the way to Cliff's house.

I inched open the door to Cliff's bedroom and found that he was snoring. I took my heels off and tiptoed into the room. I was scared as hell and totally regretted going out tonight. I slowly closed the door behind me and slid out of my tight black dress, placing it with my bag over in the closet. I crept to the bathroom and quietly closed the door. Then I locked it.

My bladder was full, and I think my nervousness made it even worse. I instantly sat on the toilet and pissed. I decided to quickly take a bird bath and grabbed a nearby washcloth, ran it under warm water in the sink, and went back to sit on the toilet. I washed my pussy while sitting on the toilet. I decided to wash under my titties and armpits too. After I was done with that, I stood up and tried to flush the toilet quietly, knowing that was impossible.

I washed my hands and patted them dry on a towel. I turned the lights off as I opened the door, and that was when I felt a hard force against my face. I fell back onto the floor. I hit my head so hard against the marble bathroom floor that my head began to spin.

My ankles were grabbed, and the grip around them was unbearable. I was dragged into the bedroom, causing me to get carpet burns. I screamed and cried out loudly. My legs were thrown, and they hit the wooden bed frame. It hurt so badly. I sat up to hold my legs where they hit the bed, and then there was a punch to my nose and I fell backward.

When I opened my eyes, Cliff was above me, on his knees. He put his hands around my neck and whispered in my ear, "Angel, you are making me turn into something we both won't be able to handle." He let my head hit the floor, and then he got up and got back in bed. I lay there with my legs and face in pain. I thought I was slick, but he was two steps ahead of me.

***

I was in the kitchen, getting the necessities to make Cliff and myself some breakfast. Cliff would be arriving from boxing practice in an hour, and I was determined to keep him happy. It would prevent me from getting my ass whupped. No one was in the house but me. Since I was alone, I decided to wear this sexy, short gown with no panties underneath. Chelsea was out in the streets, and she had invited me to come along, but I had declined.

I decided that I wouldn't go out with her until our Miami trip, which was in less than a week. She seemed to be the root of all evil with her scams and lifestyle. Even though she was a ton of fun, my body couldn't take another hit.

Tristan came into the kitchen and sat down at the table. I continued taking things out of the refrigerator for our meal. He watched my every move. After minutes and minutes of staring, he got up. My back was facing him, so I didn't see him, but I heard him. He turned me around, knelt down, went under my short gown, and slid his tongue across my pussy.

My juices started flowing, and it was almost as if I could feel them coming down my inner thigh. He stood up and stared at me. He was sexy as hell, and the look he was giving me made me want to climb on top of him. I stood there, deciding if I should take the chance or not. I mean, what were the chances of the two of us being here alone? It was the perfect opportunity.

He grabbed my hand and led me down to the basement. We ended up in the laundry room in the far back. He lifted me on top of the dryer and turned it on, which turned me on. The way it vibrated under me took me someplace else. He pulled out his dick.

"You knew you were going to fuck me?" I asked. I didn't really like the fact that he was so sure of himself. His sexy smile made me throw that thought out of my mind. I grabbed his face and started tonguing him down.

Then I grabbed his dick and put it in myself. I was thirsty for him. He lifted his right eyebrow, and I grabbed the back of his neck and started kissing him again. He started grinding me and working me slowly. It felt so good, as if his dick was made just for me. He sucked on my fingertips, and then he put my own hand on my clit. I staring playing with myself, turning him on. That made him fuck me even better. I wrapped my legs around his legs and pulled him closer to me to get his dick deeper inside me.

I let out a small moan. This felt way too good. I was still playing with myself.

"Let me lick that off your hand," he said seductively. I put my fingers in his mouth. The warmth felt so good. I started nibbling on his shoulder, and then he started pumping me hard, but still so slowly.

"Go faster," I cried.

He sped it up, and I started pulling my hair. My eyes were closed tight, but I knew when I opened them, I would see Mike . . . and I did. It was only for a split second, and before I could react, I saw Tristan with his dreads, which were no longer in a ponytail. Sweat was forming on his forehead.

I wiped it off with my hand. He was looking down, watching his dick go in and out of my pussy. When he looked up at me, biting his bottom lip, I started to lose control. My eyes rolled in the back of my head, my toes curled, and then I came.

He kissed me, and then he picked me up and placed me on the floor. He left the room and came back with a wet washcloth. I washed myself quickly. I fixed my hair, and after Trist gave me the "You look okay" nod of approval, I was set. Above us, we heard movement, meaning someone was home. I looked at Trist with fear in my eyes. I prayed it wasn't Cliff.

"If it's my brother, just say you was washing clothes. I'll stay down here for a while," he whispered. He handed me a basket of clean clothes, and I headed up the steps. When I reached the top, Cliff was there, sitting at the table.

"Baby, your home early," I said in a sweet voice.

He looked me up and down, and then he stood up. I dropped the laundry basket, hoping like hell he didn't hit me. He opened his arms, and I went to give him a hug. He rubbed on my ass.

"No panties?" he asked with a big smile.

I smiled back. I hoped sex was the last thing on his mind. He grabbed my arm and led me upstairs. I wanted to cry. I didn't think my body could take it. I had fucked his brother five minutes ago. My poor pussy couldn't take it.

He instructed me to lie down, and I begged to give him head instead, but he wanted to be inside of me. I wasn't sure if he would be able to tell that I had just got done fucking or not. If he did, I would be good as dead, and I didn't want to die.

He told me that he was going to step in the shower, and when he got out, he wanted me to be completely naked. He left the room, and I looked through the crack in the bedroom door and saw Trist blow me a kiss. It made me blush.

I got up, took my gown off, and exposed my naked body, which had the shape of a Coca-Cola bottle. Trist licked his lips. His presence made me want to fuck him again, but I had to settle for his brother, Cliff. I got back in the bed and placed my hands between my legs.

I heard Cliff coming out of the bathroom. Trist must have, too, because when I looked back out through the crack, he was gone. Cliff didn't bother drying off or anything. He just got in the bed and got between my thighs, forcing them open.

The entire process was a disaster for me, yet heaven for him. I wasn't turned on at all, and my walls kept getting dry. He had to spit on his dick repeatedly to create moisture, and I could tell that he was embarrassed by that. Obviously, it wasn't embarrassing enough to make him stop fucking me.

I thought of the good, though. I was happy because I had found a new love in this house. . . . It was Tristan's dick.

Chapter 15

When we touched down in Fort Lauderdale, the sun was beaming. We waited outside the airport for the shuttle to pick us up. All of our bodies were banging, and thus we caught the attention of every nigga at the airport.

Hanging with these two girls gave me an I'm-the-shit type of attitude. I was getting too old for that, but I wasn't the same twenty-six-year-old Angel anymore. I was twenty-two-year-old Crystal.

"Crystal, I think that's our shuttle," Beautyful said as she picked up her carry-on bag. We all grabbed our stuff as the shuttle pulled over and stopped for us.

Chelsea opened the back door and stuck her head in. "Is this for Chelsea Moore?" she asked the young Arabian driver.

"Yes, Chelsea Moore," he repeated, reading her name off of a piece of paper.

She pulled her head out of the van and said, "This is us."

As we walked over to the shuttle, a group of niggas stopped us. There were five of them. They were the same dudes that we had seen at the mall the day I snuck out. They had a Hummer limo picking them up at the airport, and I knew money definitely had something to do with that.

"Don't y'all strip?" one of the light-skinned niggas asked.

We all looked at each other, and Beautyful answered, "Yeah. Why? What's up?"

"Can y'all do a party for us at KOD on Saturday?" he asked.

"We gotta think that over, hon," Chelsea said while handing him her phone. "Put ya number in, and we'll hit you up."

Smiling at me, he told her that I already had it. I returned the smile, and then we got in the van and headed to Miami.

"Y'all know I don't, or can't, strip." I giggled.

I was sitting in the last row, while Beautyful and Chelsea were in the front row. They both glanced back at me and gave me a look that said they had an idea.

"What are y'all thinking?" I asked. I was puzzled by the facial expressions they were wearing.

"We're like a triple threat. We could get hella money," Chelsea said. She was rather convincing.

I had fallen in love with money. I also loved the attention that they were getting from the niggas, and I wanted it for myself. I figured stripping with them wouldn't hurt, but then again, I couldn't dance.

After about an hour's drive, we pulled in front of the Royal Palm Hotel at Fifteenth and Collins. There were niggas all around the hotel. I wasn't used to seeing so many niggas in one spot when there was no violence involved. Hotel employees came out and put our bags on a trolley. We went inside to check in at the front desk. There were a million niggas in there, too. There was a big white leather couch that was occupied by a few females and few males.

All eyes were on us, probably because we were wearing jeans that looked like they had been painted on us. Our nails and sew-ins were fresh, not to mention our faces, which were flawless.

After we got our room keys, we headed to the elevator. There was a bar to the left of us, and we heard a lot of the men there call, "Aye, Ma" and "Y'all bad." We ignored all of it. I had noticed that these two girls never stopped or looked at the niggas that hollered at them unless the niggas physically approached them.

We rode the elevator all the way to the twelfth floor. Our room was at the end of the hall. Chelsea slid the key in the lock, and the little bulb on the door turned green. She opened the door, and we all walked in and went straight to the balcony. The view was beautiful. You could see the beach and the tops of the palm trees from our room.

"I'm definitely fucking somebody on this," Chelsea confessed as she started laughing.

We all took turns taking showers, then changed from our travel clothes into something that would give us that Miami feel. We wanted to feel like we were at home. We put on bikinis with blue jean shorts, leaving our shorts unbuttoned and folded over. Our bikinis were all plain; mine was red, Chelsea's was yellow, and Beautyful's was blue. All of us wore heels to match our bikinis.

After relaxing in the sun at the beach, we were ready to explore the places that we had in mind. We decide to head out to King of Diamonds so that I could audition to be a dancer. The entire drive there, the girls asked me a heap load of questions.

"You nervous?" Chelsea asked.

"A little bit," I confessed. I was daydreaming about how the audition would go. These girls really had me out of my element.

"Just tune everybody out, and pretend you're dancing in a mirror," Chelsea said.

I looked at her sideways and burst out into laughter.

"I know. *The Players Club*." She laughed, knowing I had caught on that she had used a line from that movie. "But it's true."

For me, this was not a good time to recite movie lines.

We pulled up to a building that didn't strike me as one of the top strip clubs in the United States. We were on Fifth Avenue, and we could see the highway from where we were parked. We paid the taxi driver and went up to the door. When we reached the door, Chelsea and Beautyful stopped. So did I.

Beautyful turned to me. "Now, they real cool in here, but this a business, so bring ya A game," she warned.

I nodded my head. By this time, I was ready to get it all done and over with.

We walked inside the dim building. It looked much bigger inside than it did outside. It looked a lot like a warehouse. As I continued to observe the place, Beautyful went to find someone to help us. She came back with a man who looked like he was in his mid thirties. He was fine, and there was something different about him, because he didn't look very interested in any of us.

"So y'all back . . . and y'all brought a friend?" he asked.

Beautyful and Chelsea nodded their heads.

"What's ya name?" he asked me.

"That's Crystal," Chelsea said, answering for me. "And this is the co-owner of this club. King."

"Stage name?" he asked next.

I had never thought to come up with one, so I said, "How about you watch me up there and then you tell me?" I gamed. I didn't know what came over me, because I was nervous as hell, but they did say to bring my A game.

He smiled and then gestured with his hand, telling me to turn around. He wanted to see what I was working with. I did a 360 seductively. He rubbed his hands together and nodded. "So what do you wanna dance to?" he asked.

I already had my song in mind. "U.S.D.A. 'Throw This Money,'" I said as I took off my shorts and walked over to the stage. They put the song on, and I transformed myself into another person. I was rocking, popping, and dropping everything I had. I seductively untied the top of my bikini. It was still tied around my stomach.

I lifted my right titty up and licked it playfully. I decided to kick my bikini bottoms off, and then I ran over to the pole and jumped up. I kept my legs spread in the air, and I slid down slowly with my pussy in the air. The music was cut off, and I stood up on the stage, waiting for the verdict.

King looked at me with no emotion on his face. I couldn't tell if I was going to get a passing grade or an F. He signaled to me to come down to where they were sitting. I collected my items and made my way toward them. I put my bikini bottoms on and took a seat next to Chelsea.

He scratched his head. "You danced before?"

I shook my head no.

"Never?"

"No, that was my first time ever doing anything like that."

"You good," he said while nodding his head. He then told me he was going to name me Pleasure, because it was a pleasure watching me dance. I smiled.

He made the other two do a little dancing and then told us we were all hired. He also told us that there was going to be a big party for the rapper Face the next day. We told him we were going to be there.

"I'm gon' call y'all Triple Threat, 'cause together, y'all is dangerous on a nigga pockets," he said.

We laughed and headed out the door.

We ate on Ocean Drive, at T.G.I. Friday's. We talked about our auditions and how we needed to find something to wear for Face's party. I was enjoying myself already, and I couldn't wait to hit the stage to see how much money I could make.

"Let's make a bet," I said between sips of my Long Island Iced Tea.

"What?" Beautyful asked. She was cutting up her grilled chicken, trying to eat cute.

"I don't know . . . something like whoever makes the most money tomorrow night," I volunteered. I really didn't know what I was trying to say.

"Oh, I see what you trying to say," Beautyful said. "Let's do it."

Chelsea nodded, as if she was down. We all decided that since we worked at KOD, we might as well do the party that boy had asked us about earlier.

Chelsea looked through my phone. "What was his name?" she asked us. We realized he had never told it to us. "This Jeremy name must be his," she said as she looked through the caller ID list.

"Must be, 'cause it don't sound familiar," I stated.

She called him. It was crazy how they knew Chelsea and Beautyful so well, but Chelsea and Beautyful didn't know them at all. She told him where we were, and he told her not to pay for anything, because they were on their way. We patiently waited for him. When he came in, of course, he was accompanied by more niggas then he was at the airport. There were about ten of them. Jeremy and two of his companions sat down, while the rest of them stood around the table.

"So y'all gon' do my party for me?" he asked with a smile on his face. I started noticing how sexy he was. I was never really a fan of yellow boys, but he was an exception. I watched him as he watched me. His neck and arms were covered with tattoos, and that left me wondering if his chest or stomach was covered as well.

"Of course," I said in my sexy voice.

He licked his lips at me. "You gon' have to give me a special birthday dance."

"Now or later?" I asked. Right after I said that, I regretted it. The freak in me was coming out and trying to take over. I couldn't have that, because I was still a lady . . . or so I thought.

He laughed and then winked his eye at me.

After they paid for our food, we got up and left. Jeremy and I walked together. He had his arm around my waist as we walked down Ocean Drive. He was telling me how bad he wanted to fuck me, how he wanted me to give him a private party in his hotel room, and that he would pay me. I told him that I would. Hell, I wanted to fuck him, too.

***

His hotel was at the Catalina, far from where we were staying. I rode in a taxi down to his hotel, which was at Nineteenth and Collins. I walked in through the restaurant entrance. Inside, the lights were dimmed, and there were a lot of people dancing to music and hanging around the bar. The niggas were eyeing me and making all types of noises as I swished past.

I went to the elevator. A sign on it read TWO PEOPLE AT A TIME. When the elevator doors opened, I understood exactly what it meant. I put my overnight bag over my shoulder and got inside the tight elevator and rode it to the third floor. When it stopped, I got off and then walked through the dim hallway, following the sign that directed me to the 325–355 rooms.

I stopped at room 355 and knocked firmly. He opened the door, wearing nothing but boxers. He confirmed my expectations. He was tatted all over, and that immediately turned me on.

I wore a long black trench coat with lingerie underneath.

"What's under that?" he asked seductively.

I just smiled and walked over to the iPod that was sitting on a stand. I noticed it because it was lit up. The room was black and white, and there was a huge mirror leaning against a wall. I looked myself over, and then I dropped my trench coat.

"Aww, yeah, baby. You the truth," Jeremy said. I saw him behind me in the mirror. He was licking his lips and staring at my ass. I popped one cheek, and then I turned around and pushed him on the bed.

"You ready for this?" I asked him.

He nodded his head. I went into my bag and retrieved my best friend. I went back over to him and climbed on top of him.

"Take off your pants," I whispered.

I put a knife I had gotten off of one of the tables at the restaurant behind my back as I got off of him. He stood up and quickly took off his pants. Then he lay back down so that I could get back on top of him. This time I sat backward. I played with his dick and balls while he moaned, gripping my thighs.

"That's all you good for is a fuck," I heard Mike say loud and clear.

I gripped my best friend tightly.

"Fuck you!" I screamed at the top of my lungs, and then I sliced his dick off. It was like every time I fucked him, I killed him. He never died, though. He screamed. I hopped off of him and turned around to face him.

He was as cute as he was the day I met him. He was yelling something, but I was so zoned out that I couldn't hear him.

"You bitch!" he yelled. It echoed in my head. It pissed me off more and more. I lifted my knife in the air, flung it, and it landed in his chest, right where his heart was. He stopped moving, and blood came out of his mouth.

I pulled my knife out and went to rinse it off. I looked at myself in the mirror, and I was no longer Angel. I didn't look like her, and I didn't feel like her. I had lost myself loving Mike, and now he was gone. I went back into the room to give him my final words.

"I know you loved me, Mike," I cried, "And I loved you too. Why would you keep her from me, Mike? Why?" Tears formed in my eyes as I went to lie next to his dead body. I put his arm around me, and I fell asleep.

When I woke up, I screamed. Jeremy was lying there dead. I didn't know what to do. I wondered who had done this and how deep of a sleep I'd been in when they did it. Why didn't they kill me, too?

I panicked. I was covered in this man's blood.

I sat there wondering if I should call the police or leave. I covered my mouth and ran to the bathroom. I quickly opened the toilet seat and puked. I had never seen a fresh dead body.

I took off the lingerie and took a three-minute shower, barely dried off, and put my trench coat back on. I grabbed my lingerie and balled it up, then jetted out of that room. I tried to walk normally when I got off the elevator, but I was way too nervous. I kept seeing his dead body in my head. This was going to haunt me for life. After I was out of the hotel, I made my way down Collins.

I was ready to go back to Atlanta. Miami was too dangerous for me. You had to be savage to come in a hotel room and kill a man while I was lying right next to him. Why didn't I hear anything?

I made my way to our hotel fast. I bobbed and weaved the many men that grabbed my arm to get my attention. I walked through the hotel doors and saw two police officers talking to a hotel clerk. My first thought was to run out of the hotel when I saw them. I knew that would make me look suspicious.

My heart dropped.

I was the last person he was with, so that made me a suspect.

What was I going to do?

I walked past the police with caution. They both said hi to me as I made my way to the elevator. When the elevator doors closed and the elevator started going up, I let out a huge sigh. I looked down at my hands, and they were shaking. My heart was still on the ground, and I was feeling sick. This was too much of an adventure for me.

When the elevator stopped at my floor, I wondered if I should tell the girls what had happened. I didn't know if saying something about it would make them suspect that I did it or not. What if they found out and considered it suspect that I hadn't told them? I didn't think they could hold water, so I decided not to. Then again, was his death *supposed* to be a secret?

I walked up to our door, slid the key in the lock, and walked in the room. They were gone. I flopped down on the bed and looked up at the ceiling. I kicked my bag to the floor. That was when I realized that my jewelry was in there. I got up to see if the bag had tipped over. That was when I questioned my innocence in Jeremy's death.

There lay a knife with specks of blood on it.

Chapter 16

We were due to dance that night at KOD, but I wasn't in the mood. My mind was stuck on how and why that knife had got in my bag. I could have sworn I had gotten rid of one similar to it. I paced the floor. I had to hide it before the girls got back, so I took a towel out of the bathroom and picked it up. I wrapped the towel around it and put it back in my bag.

I decided to call Tiffany to talk to my little sister. The phone rang four times before she finally answered.

"Yes?" she said, sounding like she had an attitude.

"Where's Crystal?" I asked.

"She's not here! Damn!" she yelled before hanging up.

I grew angry and was just about ready to fly to Chicago to whup her ass. I decided to call back.

"Look, Angel, you really need to seek help and quit calling my phone," she politely told me, and then she hung up again. I sat on the bed, looking at my phone in shock. First, Mike tried to keep me from my daughter, and now Tiffany was trying to pull the same move with my sister. I had too much on my mind.

Chelsea and Beautyful came in about two hours later, talking loudly. They both had a margarita in a big glass in their hand.

"Have you heard from Jeremy?" Beautyful asked. Her glass was almost empty, so she poured some of Chelsea's drink into it.

"Not since I left him this morning," was my response. I didn't know why I lied. I guess it felt like the truth would just backfire on me.

"Where the hell did you go bright and early this morning?" Chelsea laughed. She was suspecting that I had ended up with another nigga.

"I was with him, but he wasn't there when I woke up." I made up a time. "I woke up around nine this morning." I looked at my bag and then back at them. "Why you ask?"

Chelsea started to tell me that the housekeeper had found him dead in his room. The police didn't know who did it or when, but they were investigating. I just sat there like I was in shock and it was my first time hearing about it. All I could see was his dead body covered in blood.

We all decided that we should get out and find us something to wear to the club. Platinum recording artist Face was going to be present. I thought to myself, *If he is any finer in person than he is on TV, then I am in trouble.* I tried to shake the whole Jeremy/Crystal thing out of my mind as we headed out to stroll the streets of Miami.

Chelsea said that she had talked to the owner of KOD, and the theme was "Thongs and Teddies." We ended up going to Victoria's Secret to look for the sets that were best for each of us. A black-and-red teddy with the matching thong caught my eye.

Chelsea came walking my way. She got up close and whispered in my ear. "You seem like you got something on your mind."

I faked a smile. "I'm cool," I sighed. Then tears fell from my eyes. I felt horrible. I told her that I just wanted to be left alone. She acted as if she understood me, and then she went on her way.

My mind was racing at full speed, and I had a gut feeling that I would be the one blamed for Jeremy's death. I kept feeling like something or somebody was trying to set me up.

Once we all found what we would wear that night, we headed back to our hotel to pack up. I went to the bathroom with my overnight bag under my arm. Something kept telling me that those two girls had been going through my bag during the course of our trip, and I wasn't having that. After I showered, I dug in my bag for my favorite body spray, and my hand stumbled across something. I slowly pulled out the object, then dropped it on the floor and screamed at the top of my lungs. Someone tried to open the bathroom door. I realized I had locked it.

"You okay?" Beautyful asked, still jiggling the doorknob.

I took a deep breath. "Yeah, I'm fine. I just saw a spider."

I grabbed a towel and picked up Jeremy's dick. Somebody had cut it off and put it in my bag. I thought about flushing it down the toilet, but I knew it would probably clog the damn thing up. I wrapped it up in the towel, and all I could think of was putting it back in my bag and getting rid of the bag altogether. I sat on the toilet and cried. Someone was really trying to send me to jail, but who and why?

When I walked out of the bathroom, they were both waiting for me, staring at me. I had a feeling they had been talking about me, and I hated being judged. Mostly, I hated being the topic of a discussion that I wasn't a part of.

Just then there were a few loud knocks on the door. We all looked at each other to see who was going to answer it. None of us were expecting company. I sat down on the bed, pretty much letting the two of them know that I definitely wasn't going to be the one to answer the door.

Beautyful decided to be the bigger person and answer it. She looked out the peephole and looked back at Chelsea. "It's your brother."

My heart hit the floor. All of my bones started to shake. I knew I was a dead woman. I was supposed to be visiting Chelsea's granny with Chelsea. Cliff hadn't called to check up on me, I had concluded that he was convinced that I was too afraid to disobey him.

Chelsea looked at me with pity all over her face. She got up and slowly walked to the door. She opened it, and her whole mood shifted.

"Trist, what are you doing here?" she asked.

You could tell she was smiling by the way she sounded. My heart lifted, and I started breathing again. Trist walked in, with his dreads hanging to his shoulders, wearing his basketball shorts with a wife beater, showing off that body. He smiled at me as he walked past and sat down on the other bed. No longer did I want to go to the club. If I suddenly backed out, I knew the girls would know it was because of him. Even though

Chelsea had told me that she didn't care what I decided to do, I doubted that fucking her other brother was one of those things.

"Y'all ready?" Chelsea asked. She started grabbing her stuff and heading to the door.

"Where y'all going?" Trist asked her.

She told him we were headed out to work.

He raised his brow. "You working too?" he asked me.

Chelsea answered yeah for me, causing him to instantly get upset. He told her she shouldn't turn out everybody that she crossed paths with. She told him to mind his own business and that I was grown and could make my own decisions.

They argued about me like I wasn't even present. I sat back and watched the show. I really wanted to stay with Trist, but then again, I wanted to see Face. This was a once-in-a-lifetime opportunity. Trist wasn't worth it.

Chelsea told me to stay and said that if I wanted to come to the club later, to catch a cab. I was fine with that because I needed some dick to get my stress level down. After I put Trist to bed, I would head to the club to make a few dollars.

As soon as they were out of sight, Trist came over to my bed and began kissing me on my neck.

"What made you come here?" I asked him, pulling his beater off.

"You," he responded. He slid my shorts off and saw that I didn't have on any panties. He looked at me, and I smiled. He dived face-first into my pussy.

I lay back and enjoyed him. Despite my enjoyment, Jeremy kept popping up in my head. Even Crystal's innocent face popped up. Tears rolled down my face.

Trist came up from down below. "Why you crying?" He wiped my tears and started putting his shirt back on.

"What are you doing?" I asked.

"You crying and shit," he said, as if I should have known why he stopped.

"No." I grabbed his arm. "I don't half step."

He looked at me to see if I was sure. Without a doubt, I was. He took his shirt back off and picked up where we had left off. He pulled his dick out and slid it in. I moaned. It felt too good. It was almost as if it belonged there. I was so wrapped up in fucking him. I was a lazy lover when it came to Trist. He slowly stroked and talked to me the entire time.

"How that feel?" he would whisper, nibbling on my ear.

"Good," I would moan.

Then he was twirling his dick inside of me. I loved it when he did that. The more we fucked, the more I fell in love with his dick. He looked me in the eyes while holding my legs all the way back, and I saw my first love.

It was Mike, but it was the lovable, young, fourteen-year-old Mike.

We were at Tiffany's, having the time of our lives. Everything about us was innocent. He started kissing me on my neck and then sucking on it. After he was done with that, he blew on it and made my body tingle. I was running my hands through his braids, and he was fucking me how I liked it. I couldn't believe I was fucking him, knowing my mother was only across the street. He had popped up over here, and I knew he hadn't come just to see me. We both knew what we wanted. Tiffany and Nicole had walked to the store and had left the two of us alone.

"I'm about to cum," he whispered.

"Okay," I said. I felt him getting weak as he pressed his body up against mine. Then he went limp on top of me. I wrapped my arms around him. "I love you, Mike."

He lifted his head up and gave me the deadliest look. I was confused. Where did Mike go? Tristan got up off of me with his eyes still on me.

"What you just say?" he asked. His voice let me know that he dared me to say it again.

I sat silent for a second. "What do you mean? I didn't say anything," I said, making him feel like he was the crazy one. I knew for sure that I had just fucked Mike. I didn't know where he had gone or when he had left, but I was certain I had. I'd felt him, I'd talked to him, and I'd held him.

Tristan didn't say anything. He went to the bathroom and closed the door. I got up and searched the room to see if Mike had left anything. He was good about leaving a shirt or a hat behind. It had been years since Mike and I had had anything, and here I was, back open.

After looking high and low, I realized he had played me for a fool again. I was disgusted, and I prayed I wouldn't cross paths with him, because I would probably spit in his face. I sat on the bed and cried. He had done what he was best at. Fucking me and leaving me.

Trist came out of the bathroom a few moments later. By then I had finished crying. I had dried the tears on my face, but my eyes were bloodshot. I had my head down, and he sat right next to me.

He put his hand on my back. "You know I came in you, right?"

I shook my head yeah. I really didn't give a fuck if he did or didn't. I was too hurt to care. He lifted up my face and saw that I was crying.

"What's wrong?"

"You wouldn't understand," I told him.

I went to the bathroom to freshen up. Afterward, I grabbed my bag and bolted out the door. I heard Trist asking me where I was going, but I ignored him and continued to run. I was headed to meet Miami's heat and to get paid at KOD. A lot of lame-ass niggas hooted and hollered at me on my way out of the hotel. My mind wasn't on them. I went outside and flagged down a cab. When I finally got one to stop, I instructed him to take me to King of Diamonds.

The cab pulled up to the club, and I hopped out. On my way to the employee dressing room, I saw King. He stopped me.

"I thought you backed out," he said. He was wearing an expensive off-white suit. With all the money floating around in this club, I was sure he had money to blow, so why not wear it?

"Naw. Family business," I responded.

He got into asking me if I wanted to dance onstage or just do lap dances for the night, and I assured him that I wasn't a half stepper.

"Put me on the stage," I said.

He cracked a smile, letting me know he felt my drive, and then we went our separate ways.

When I entered the dressing room, I saw the hate-filled eyes and all the jealous smirks. I ignored them and continued on my way. I went to the back of the dressing room to get dressed. When I was done, I got up and went to join the party.

I had on a crotchless black leather thong with a matching bra. My black and diamond stilettos clicked against the tile floor as I walked down the long hall to reach the party. It was like everything was in slow motion. Why had I considered stripping? I had been a boring person throughout my life. Now I looked different, dressed different, and was acting different. Who was I?

Before I could answer my own question, I was already at the party. The club was packed, and there were niggas in every direction. There was nothing but money, niggas, and hoes, and since I was there, I had to pick a category. I saw a table with three guys. There was no one there entertaining them, so I decided to make my way over to them.

When I reached their table, I started grinding my hips on the one who looked like he had the most money. He was dark skinned and looked a lot older. . . . Maybe he was a little too old to be rocking gold jewelry. He had on dark shades, so I couldn't see his eyes, but it wasn't like I needed to see them in order to see his money. I moved my head from side to side to the music and let my body go with the flow.

He never touched me. I did notice that he had to keep stopping himself from doing so. The more I ground on his dick, the hornier I got. He and his boys had a pile of money on the table for me. I decided since they were all paying, why not entertain the other two?

I got off of Mr. Gold and headed to his friend who was to the left of him. He was fine. I saw Chelsea across the room, shaking her ass in front of some nigga. I couldn't tell who. I was hoping it wasn't Face. My bangs were in my eyes. I moved them behind my ear and realized exactly who he was. He was Omar.

I was hurt. I grabbed my money and quickly walked away.

Gold got up and followed me. I could feel him on my heels. What the hell did he want? I thought. It was nothing to get another girl to dance. He grabbed my arm and turned me around. I could tell he was looking deep into my eyes behind those glasses.

"You look familiar," he said.

I stood there, silent. I was hoping he didn't mean I looked like the criminal who was on the news in Chicago. He had a grill in his mouth, and it gleamed from the lights. He was wearing True Religion blue jeans and a tee. He had on some gator shoes and every piece of jewelry you could wear. As I stared at his face, I read the side of his shades. Those were Gucci frames covering his eyes.

"Why you leave?" he asked after realizing I had no explanation.

"I had to," I said. I was surprised that the music wasn't playing as loudly where we were. He grabbed my face. "Angel?"

I moved my head to get him to let me go. I walked away. He stood where I had left him, and hollered my name. I didn't know who this man was or how he knew me. I was running away from being Angel, and here this man was bringing her right back to me.

I went into the dressing room. I had totally panicked. Although I wanted to go snatch Omar from under Chelsea's ass, I couldn't attract attention. I sat down on one of the wooden benches in the dressing room and put my head down. I needed to leave Miami. It was too risky for someone to know who I was. I couldn't have that. I got up and began grabbing my things and stuffing them in my bag.

King walked in. "Pleasure," he called.

I turned around to face him.

"Where you going?" he asked with his hands up.

I just shook my head. I had a knot in my throat and wouldn't be able to say a word without crying.

He began telling me that my girls were out there and Face was asking to see the Triple Threat. I didn't want to mess up what they had planned, so I put my bag down and headed back out. I saw King do some hand gesture to the DJ.

"Here's the other member of Triple Threat. Pleasure! You niggas won't be disappointed, so get up and make it rain on Beautyful, Luxury, and Pleasure!" the DJ yelled into the mic.

We all got on the stage, and I must have forgotten that Omar was present. However, I was reminded when I saw him front and center in the crowd. I instantly grew nervous.

I already knew that my surgery hadn't provided the best disguise, being that a man I didn't even know knew exactly who I was. The beat dropped, and so did our clothes. All the guys were getting closer to the stage. Some wanted to see us up close, while others just wanted to sneak touches. I was numb.

I saw Omar throwing all types of cash at Chelsea, who was at the other end of the stage. I looked over in disgust. I climbed the pole and did a trick on my way down. I wanted his attention, but Chelsea had it all.

After my attempt to get Omar's attention, I noticed two guys, who I assumed were detectives, come through the doors. They both were black and tall. One looked younger than the other. My heart sank. My first thought was to jump from the stage and go to the dressing room. I was stuck. As I rolled my hips, I watched the detectives through my peripheral vision.

They were talking to King, and then he started pointing at me. The detectives made their way over to the stage and gestured for me to go over to them. I walked over to them slowly and knelt down.

"Someone is looking for you," the older one said directly in my ear.

"Now?" I asked.

He shook his head yeah.

I climbed from the stage and followed him. "Can I at least put my clothes on?" I yelled.

He shook his head no as we walked outside. There was a Hummer limo sitting there, and I had a weird feeling it was Cliff. Damn, I was dead. I tried to come up with every excuse in the book as to why I needed to go back in. They weren't hearing it.

The younger one opened the limo door, and I slowly climbed inside. He slammed the door behind me, and to my surprise, there sat Face. He was looking like a million bucks. His diamonds were sparkling from the dim lights in the ceiling. He had a bottle of Hennessy in his left hand and his iPhone in the other. His smooth caramel skin glistened. The many tattoos that covered his arms and hands complemented his swag.

I was in awe.

"Thought you was going to jail, huh?" He chuckled.

I nodded my head as I made my way to the back of the limo, where he was sitting. He smiled as he watched me crawl seductively over the seats to reach him.

"Yeah, I been watching you like a hawk, and you got what I want," he said as he licked his lips. He took a drink from his bottle.

"You got what I want, too," I responded, referring to his money.

He laughed and then grabbed me softly. I stood up and began giving him a lap dance. It was evident to me he wanted a dance. It was also evident that he wanted to fuck. I was positive he knew I wanted money. We would satisfy each other.

When did he see me? I wondered, because I hadn't seen him inside the club. He got up, put his bottle on the counter, and locked the limo doors. Then he sat by the door.

"Come walk down here like a model," he demanded. He was having fun.

I smiled and began strutting my stuff. The whole way to him, I wondered how big his dick was, or if it was even big at all. When I made it to him, he grabbed a handful of my ass.

"Now fuck me without fucking me." He smacked my ass, and I seductively turned around and did what I thought was fucking him without actually fucking him. I started grinding my ass on his dick, and then I began popping on it. I had no music. In my head, I was listening to Trey Songz's "On Top."

There was a bar above our heads. I grabbed ahold of it and lifted myself up, managing to do an acrobatic split on top of him. He began to lick his lips and rub on my body. After I straddled him and started sucking on his neck, he untied my top and exposed my titties. He grabbed one and starting sucking away. After a little bit of that, he whispered in my ear.

"I'm ready."

I was confused. What the hell was he ready for? So I asked, "For what?" I was still grinding on him at this point.

"To fuck you," he stated, as if I should have known.

I said, "Okay."

He told the driver to take us to his mansion.
As we headed to his mansion, which stood by the
water, he continued licking on me and fingering
me. He repeatedly told me how ready he was to
fuck me. As bad as I wanted to fuck him, I was
growing tired of him telling me that. I figured it
was the liquor talking.

We pulled up to a gated community. He rolled
his window down and punched in a code. The
gates slowly opened. We turned down a few
streets, and then we were pulling up to a big-ass
white house. We came to a complete stop. Ten
seconds later the limo driver opened the door
for us. I followed Face's lead and headed to the
house.

Chapter 17

When we got inside his home, we went directly to the first bedroom to our right. There was a huge round bed with satin Fendi sheets and mirrors on the ceiling. There was a pole across from the bed, with a light shining down on it. I decided to jump on it and show him a thing or two. Where my pole game skills came from, I had no idea. Angel knew nothing about climbing a pole.

I climbed the pole, and I slid down with my feet above my head. He sat down on the bed with his half-empty bottle of Henny in his hand. The more tricks I did, the hornier he got. He eventually told me to just come over and get in the bed. I did so. He took his clothes off and leaned back. He handed me a condom, and I put it on his dick. Being that I was dressed in a crotchless outfit, I decided to just mount him.

I began riding him, and he immediately started smacking my ass. I wasn't used to getting my ass smacked within a minute of fucking, but I went along with the flow. He grabbed my titties and nibbled on them one at a time. I loved the feeling. We changed positions and went straight to doggy style. He spread my ass cheeks and starting grinding his dick inside of me. I gripped the sheets and bit them at the same time. His dick game was on point. He grabbed a fistful of my hair as he sped up his pace. I tried to run, because he was just too much for me. Again, he smacked my ass.

"Where you going? Throw that shit back." He smacked my ass again.

After a while, I felt like he was trying to prove a point, or maybe that was just how he fucked. He pulled his dick out and flipped me around. I looked in his eyes, and it was Mike. He got up off the bed and went into another room. When he came back, he had some handcuffs and a bottle of champagne. He set them both down on the nightstand that was right next to where my head was lying.

I figured Mike was trying to kidnap me or maybe kill me. I refused to let him kill me. I had to do something and quick! I looked out the window. It was still dark. My eyes roamed to the TV stand, and I noticed a small black object sitting on it. It had a red light, but I couldn't see exactly what it was.

He handed me the handcuffs and then slid his dick back inside of me. He was giving me all he had as his balls slapped up against my ass. I clenched the cuffs tightly, and then I laid them on the bed. I watched him closely. He was too busy fucking the daylights out of me to even notice my movements.

I started fake moaning. "Yes, Daddy, right there," I said as I inched my hand to the champagne bottle. "Take this pussy." When the bottle was finally in my hand, I lifted it over my head and cracked him upside the head.

He fell over, unconscious.

I got up and handcuffed his left wrist to the handle of the nightstand. I searched the room for something to finish this bastard off with. I threw everything he had on and the bottle into the bedroom closet. I made sure to put it on a shelf that was down on the floor so that no one could see it. I stumbled upon something. I picked it up and stared at it. A revolver.

"Hmm, now look here," I said to the gun. I left the closet and headed back to Mike. He was still out cold. I flipped his body over so that he was facing the ceiling.

"I always loved you, Mike, I really did, but it was like you took my love for granted," I confessed, with the gun aimed at his dick. I pulled the trigger. *Pow!* His body jerked, and mine did too. Blood seeped from his dick.

Now I knew he would never be able to fuck anyone else. I still wasn't satisfied.

"Where is she?" I screamed. I sat down on the bed and pressed the gun against his head. "Where the fuck is she!" I knew I wouldn't get an answer out of him, but I still expected one.

I stood up and aimed the gun right in the middle of his forehead and pulled the trigger again. He was better dead than alive. I backed away from him, until my back was up against the wall. I slid down and started crying.

It was our last day in Miami, and we decided that we would go to a club instead of working at KOD. We all decided to try Club Mansion, since it was the most popular club to be in. They said the club had at least eight dance floors, and I wanted to see if that was true.

We were watching BET while taking turns showering. The news came on and interrupted our show. "Breaking news. Here in South Beach, Florida, rapper and music mogul Anthony Face Hudson was murdered in his own home yesterday. Officials are unsure who did this hideous crime, but his limo driver said he last saw the rapper with a dancer from the top strip club King of Diamonds. So far that is all we know," a short, black-haired lady said.

We all sat there quietly, and when I searched the room with my eyes, Beautyful and Chelsea were staring at me. Their expressions told me that they felt I did it . . . but I didn't. I hadn't even known the man was dead.

"Crystal, what the fuck is going on? Seriously." Chelsea had fear all over her face.

I shook my head, because I honestly didn't have a clue. I couldn't believe that they would think that I was capable of killing someone.

"Somebody is trying to set me up," I cried. My eyes were full of tears. I was innocent, and here they were, sitting here and judging me. I had no proof that I didn't kill him, but they had no proof that I did. I *did* remember leaving the club with him and fucking him in his bed, but that was all.

"You need to let us know what really happened. I mean, let us know so that we can help you," Chelsea begged.

I could tell she was scared of me. Hell, I was scared of me too. Did I really kill him and Jeremy, or was someone trying to frame me? I just didn't know who would want to do this to me.

"Chelsea, I don't know," I said, scared about how this would all turn out.

"We need to leave before they come find you and take you down for questioning," Beautyful suggested, facing in Chelsea's direction.

Chelsea nodded her head, agreeing with her.

We gathered all of our things and reserved a taxi to pick us up within the next hour. Here I was, running again. We left out hotel room and took the elevator down, and on our way out to the taxi, we noticed three police officers in the lobby. They were talking to the lady at the front desk. My heart sank, and I knew for sure I'd been caught this time.

We all engaged in a conversation so as not to seem suspicious or scared. We passed the officers safely and were out the door. The receptionist handed the police a room key, and they headed over to the elevators. We jumped in the first taxi we saw.

"To the Fort Lauderdale airport please," Beautyful directed.

The older black man looked in his mirror and smiled at us.

"Perv," Chelsea mumbled as we pulled off.

As I sat between the two of them, I felt like a convict trying to get to the border of Mexico. I couldn't believe I was at this point in my life again. Where could I have gone wrong?

The ride to Fort Lauderdale took almost an hour. They both fell asleep. I was afraid that we were going to get pulled over, and I didn't want to be asleep when that happened. It seemed like every time I closed my eyes, I saw Jeremy's dead body covered in blood.

I missed my little sister and Omar dearly. Damn, I couldn't believe Omar had let Chelsea's funky ass dance all over him. I kind of wondered if I would ever see him again. I prayed I would, that is, if I didn't wind up in jail first. My mind was all over the place. I tried not to think negatively, but I couldn't help it in this situation. My phone vibrated in my hand. It was Cliff. He hadn't called me this entire trip, and now, all of a sudden, he was calling. I decided not to answer.

When we pulled up to the airport, I shook them until they woke up. We paid the driver and grabbed our bags out of the car. I decided to leave my overnight bag behind, afraid that if I didn't get rid of that penis and knife, I would get busted in the metal detector. We got in line and waited to check our bags. My phone vibrated again. This time it vibrated a little lighter. That let me know that I had a text message.

I'm going to kill you, it read.

It was from Cliff. I instantly got the chills. I figured he was home and wondering where I was. I didn't answer, so there was no telling where he thought I could be. I was digging myself into a deeper hole by the minute.

As we got closer to the scale to weigh our luggage, I saw two familiar faces. I had to zoom in with my eyes, because they had to be playing tricks on me. The two individuals were accompanied by a little girl who appeared to be four or five years old.

Mike and Nicole walked past me, and then they stopped. My mouth hit the floor. This bitch was sleeping with my man. Mike looked the same. Nothing had changed about him. Nicole looked the same, too, except for the fact that she had gained a little bit of weight over the years.

"Nicole, when did you two start dating?" I questioned.

"Excuse me? Do we know you?"

"Angel."

"Angel?" Nicole asked, as if she wasn't really sure it was me or not. I wanted to spit on this trifling bitch. If looks could kill, they would both be good as dead.

Chelsea grabbed my arm to stop me from walking up to them.

Beautyful whispered in my ear. "Your name is Crystal," she reminded me. I was upset that I had almost forgot I was a wanted woman.

"No. Sorry," I replied. The tears welled up in my eyes. Seeing my first love and one of my good friends together like they were a couple was heartbreaking. Nicole gave me a look that told me she thought that I was crazy. I was at a loss for words. No words could justify how I felt, anyway, so I kept quiet. Another tear dropped from my eye.

"Who was that?" Chelsea asked. She was concerned.

I wiped my eyes and shook my head. They were nobody, and I had to remember that. I walked up to the scale to weigh my bag. If only this scale could weigh my heart, I was sure it weighed a hundred pounds more than normal.

Walking out of prison a free man after all those years was going to feel refreshing to Albert. It would be a weird feeling to be free to roam without someone telling him that he was going too far.

Porsha was sitting in her Honda Civic, awaiting Albert's release. She was happier than a little kid in a candy store. She had life figured out. She and Albert would get married and live happily after ever. Little did she know, Albert had no intention of being with her. He was determined to find Sarah and try to rekindle those old flames.

He said his good-byes to his fellow inmates, spoke a few harsh words to the guards, and walked through the gate and into the lobby. He walked up to the front desk with the glass wall in front of it. A younger Caucasian woman sat inside the enclosure.

"I need my stuff, lady. Albert Christopher Jacobs." He began hitting the glass with his hand.

"I heard you," she said as she entered his name into the computer. She went to retrieve his belongings and came back with a midsize orange envelope that read INMATE #30-6714. She quickly slid the glass window open and handed it to him, then quickly shut the window.

He looked inside the envelope and realized he didn't have shit worth keeping. Inside, there was a set of keys and three hundred dollars. He knew the keys held no value, so he threw them away, then pocketed the money and walked out the door.

He knew his young thing would be sitting outside waiting for him as he'd instructed. He had it all figured out. He would use her up until she had nothing left. She was a pawn to him, and he was sure she could lead him to his checkmate.

He smiled as he got closer to the car. She was all smiles. She was excited, horny, and ready for whatever. She embraced him, and he picked her up off of the ground and spun her around. She kissed his neck and told him how much she had missed him.

"I missed you too," he told her. He went around to the driver's side and opened the car door for her. She was swept off of her feet already. A guy had never opened a door for her. He closed it behind her and went over and got in on the passenger's side. She was beyond happy. She couldn't stop herself from smiling.

He looked at her and shook his head in pity. She was so naive. She kind of reminded him of his baby mama, Teresa, in terms of how easily convinced they both were. He loved nothing more than to have a strong woman with a strong mind.

"I need you to take me somewhere, but first I need to go get a shovel," he told her, thinking about that money he had hidden years ago. He prayed that it was still there and that he still remembered where he'd buried it.

Porsha hoped he wasn't getting the shovel to bury Angel. He had just gotten out, and she was certain that Angel could never have made him that mad. He had just gotten out of jail and was already dying to go right back. She hoped and prayed that Cliff had everything straight on his end. She hadn't talked to him in almost a month.

She stopped at the Home Depot so that Albert could purchase a shovel. This day was not going how she had envisioned it. She had thought that they were going to go out to eat and then go home and go at it like rabbits, but he was only thinking about himself. She should have known that he was just like the rest of them. While she waited in the car for him to return, she decided to call Cliff to see how things were with him and Angel.

"Yo," Cliff answered after the second ring.

"How are things?" she asked, getting straight to the point.

Cliff was fed up with Angel's disobedient ass. He was ready to kill her himself. He had a terrible anger problem, for which he had sought out help years ago. She was making it worse. He truly cared about her, but when Juice, Face's limo driver, called him and told him that he had just dropped Angel and Face off at his mansion, Cliff was infuriated. She'd been too busy being a ho to realize that Juice was the same man who had driven them around when he came to Chicago. Cliff had sent Juice a picture of Angel's transformation after her surgery. Juice already knew that she was Cliff's alleged girlfriend, and he and Face thought it would get Cliff off his high horse, if Face seduced her.

Cliff had sworn up and down that his girl was in North Carolina with his sister, but after Juice sent him a picture of the King of Diamonds flyer featuring Angel, Chelsea, and Beautyful, he knew no lie was being told. He really wanted to fly to Miami and beat her ass on the stage, but he couldn't have the media in his business.

He had never thought Angel was the type, but with Chelsea in her ear, she was good as gone. Juice had even said that he had one of their boys set up a camera because they were on their way to Face's house. Cliff's blood had boiled over when he heard this news. Whether he saw the video or not, he was going to beat Angel nearly to death, not because she cheated, but because she had embarrassed him.

With that in mind, he simply said, "It's going."

"Well, Albert is out. I don't know when he wants to get his hands on her, but I'm sure it'll be sooner rather than later," Porsha said with certainty.

"Okay, cool. Just see when he's talking, and leave the rest to me." Cliff was going to beat Angel's ass before she was laid to rest. He had never let a bitch get away with making him look stupid, and he wasn't going to start. Here he was, housing this ungrateful criminal, and she was giving him her ass to kiss.

He hung up his phone and flicked the TV on. He had been sitting on the couch, looking at the TV screen for over an hour. He'd flown home from Vegas early, after hearing the news about Angel. The information had really affected him. He'd told himself he didn't love her, but if he didn't, why was he hurt? Love was pain, and he was going to love the pain he made Angel feel.

As we landed, I was praying that Cliff was not home. I already knew what the repercussions would be like. I knew I shouldn't have listened to Chelsea's dumb ass, because she sure as hell wasn't going to help me or get him off of me when he attacked me.

The drive home seemed to have flown past. Before I knew it, we were pulling up to the house. I prolonged getting out of the car. As I held on to my bags, I dragged my feet to the door. Chelsea and Beautyful were in the house at least ten minutes before I got there.

When I walked through the door, Cliff was standing at the foot of the stairs with a belt in his hand. I wanted to turn back around and run until my feet went numb. I didn't want to take my bags upstairs, nor did I want to get my ass beat in front of them. I looked at Chelsea, who was sitting in the living room. She mouthed the word *sorry*. Sorry wasn't going to change anything.

I decided to face him and get it over with. As I passed him, he gave me an evil look. He followed me up the stairs, saying anything that came to his mind. I got butterflies in my stomach. I figured this wasn't going to go as planned.

I walked slowly into the bedroom, and he pushed me, trying to help me speed up the process. I turned around and slapped him with my bag. He stumbled and fell down, and then I tried to run past him. He grabbed me and threw me to the floor. I knew I was dead.

The belt had fallen from his hand when I hit him with my luggage. He stood up and picked it up. He wrapped it around his fist and started beating me with the buckle. I balled up in a fetal position. The hits pierced my skin as the buckle landed and left welts. I screamed and I cried, but I knew he didn't care about me. At that moment I wished I was in jail. At least I would have been safe from him.

When he finally got tired, he threw the belt at me and walked out of the room. I stayed on the floor, weakened. I had doubts that I could even stand up. The pain was too excruciating. Moments later Beautyful and Chelsea came running in. They both crouched on the floor and started asking me if I was okay. It was obvious that I wasn't, so I didn't say a word. They both helped me up and carried me to the bed.

Chelsea left the room, and Beautyful stayed at my side. She looked around the room, making sure the coast was clear. "You need to leave him alone," she whispered, as if I didn't know that already.

I nodded. I felt her 100 percent. She began telling me how she was close to the girl that used to date Cliff and how he broke her all the way down. She explained how their business was all over the media, which was more embarrassing than anything. She also told me that Chelsea was nothing but a conniving bitch. Every time she brought a new stripper to King of Diamonds, *she* got paid something extra.

Chelsea was all about the money and could have cared less about me. She was the one who had introduced Beautyful to the fast life and the reason she had lost herself in this lifestyle. She so badly wanted to change, but she couldn't stay away from the fast money. She told me if I had any common sense, I would run away and never look back.

She hugged me and left the room. As I lay there, I replayed everything she had told me. I did want to run away, but I had nowhere to go and nobody to run to. With an aching body and head, I managed to fall asleep.

While Angel slept, Chelsea and Cliff sat in the living room, talking.

"Now, why you have to do her like that?" Chelsea asked.

Cliff shook his head. His mind was too far gone. He had come to the realization that he loved Angel. She had humiliated him, and she needed to be punished. Chelsea knew better than anyone that he didn't allow his women to disrespect him in any way, shape, or form.

"Disrespectful. Why you take her there?" he questioned her.

She shrugged her shoulders and told him that she'd wanted to go. He knew better than that, though. He knew how convincing and manipulative his sister could be to a naive girl like Angel.

Their conversation was interrupted by the doorbell. Cliff got up to get the door, and Chelsea got up to go upstairs. He looked through the peephole, and to his surprise, it was Juice. This kind of threw him for a loop, being that Juice was supposed to be in Miami, working for Face. When he opened the door, Juice stood there, distraught. He invited Juice in. He noticed that he had a camera in his hand. Cliff was hoping like hell that he didn't come all the way to Atlanta to show him the tape of Face fucking Angel.

Cliff shut the door and followed behind Juice, who went straight to the living room. He didn't say a word. Instead, he sat down and stared into space.

"What's up, dude?" Cliff asked. At this point, he was beginning to wonder if he'd seen Face fucking his bitch on the camera. Juice remained silent. He handed Cliff the camera. Cliff turned it on, and about ten videos were lined up across the screen. One was from yesterday, so he decided to watch that first.

He took a seat. He knew he wasn't going to be able to handle whatever was on the camera, especially if Angel was involved. The video started with somebody running past the camera, and then Face went over to the bed to sit, watching. Then he saw Angel make her way to him. He started to turn off the camera, but something made him want to see more. He watched them fuck, and then the video showed Face leaving the room. He came back with a bottle of champagne and something shiny.

Juice was looking down, and Cliff wondered why. He continued to watch. He watched as Angel reached for the bottle with her delicate hands, then hit Face upside his head. Cliff couldn't believe that the rest of the video was actually of her. She appeared to be innocent and harmless, but she was a malicious murderer. The way she pulled the trigger of the revolver she found, without a thought of remorse, shocked him. She was a totally different person on the video than she was when he was around her.

He couldn't hear everything she was saying, but he could hear her calling Juice Mike. Cliff was almost certain that Mike wasn't Face's government name. She aimed the gun at his head and let a bullet loose. This made Cliff jump a little. This bitch was nuts and belonged in a psych ward if you asked him. She was really crazy. He didn't see Face do anything that would give her a reason to want to kill him. He was at a loss for words as he gave Juice the camera.

Juice sat there, shaking his head. He didn't know what to do. He knew who had killed his friend, but he wasn't a snitch, so he couldn't tell. He wondered whether this counted as dropping a dime. It wasn't like Angel was affiliated with any gang or set, so would the hood care if he told the Feds who had killed one of the best hip-hop artists out there?

"I know what you thinking, and you can't tell," Cliff said, still shaken by what he had just watched.

As bad as he wanted Angel's crazy ass out of his house at this point, he knew that her dad was going to kill her soon. He had money on the line, and Juice wasn't going to take that away. He decided to let him in on the little deal he had with Albert. Maybe that would make him want to hold water. He told him that if he kept quiet, he would give him ten racks, half of what he was getting. At least that was what he told Juice.

Juice agreed. He loved Face, but the money was worth keeping quiet for a little while. Cliff told Juice to give him the camera, because he wanted to be sure that he wouldn't say a word. Juice handed it to Cliff without any problem and headed out the door.

Cliff knew from that point on he would be sleeping with one eye open. He figured he'd better go make up with her. Although he was stronger than her, it was obvious strength had nothing to do with it when it came to her. Angel was no angel at all.

Chapter 18

Albert was growing tired of Porsha's clingi-ness. She wanted to be under him 24/7, and to him that was way too much. He liked her to an extent, but not enough to be around her all the time. After she saw how much money he had dug up from the back of Teresa's old house, she really didn't want to let him loose.

He'd had three hundred thousand dollars buried in her backyard for all those years. It was untouched, and he needed every penny. He had been saving his money for years, and after getting a settlement from an accident he was in years ago, it put him up in the money game.

He knew he would need it for a rainy day, but he never imagined that going to jail would be the rain. His mind was set on getting his hands on Angel and her lying-ass mama. He sat on Por-sha's full-sized bed in her little apartment, deep in thought. Porsha came out of the bathroom and sat on the bed next to him.

"What's on your mind?" She had on a tight tiger-print shirt that made her titties pop out.

Albert looked at her. "Where's Angel?"

She told him that Angel was in Atlanta with Cliff, that she knew exactly where she was, and that he didn't need to worry. She told him to let her handle it and to trust her. Albert nodded his head. He didn't trust himself, so trusting her was out of the question. He didn't have any plans to get Teresa, but after pondering the matter for a long time, he thought, *Why not kill her too?* She was the one who had made Angel talk to the police, and she'd also made her act dumb when they were doing that study on her. Teresa had been loud in the courtroom, telling them that Albert had caused Angel to develop a serious illness. That was when they decided to do a study on her. When the results came back, they agreed that he had indeed messed her up in the head. That was when the judge decided that he didn't deserve to get credit for his time spent behind bars.

He told Porsha that he needed to see her car because he had to make a run. She was reluctant at first, but she wasn't going to tell him no. He took the keys to her Honda and headed to Teresa's house. No one knew when he was getting out, so he knew that showing up at Teresa's door was going to shock her. She had lived in the same house forever.

He didn't know what he had seen in her. She'd been a cute young girl, but she too was clingy. He had told her up front that he had a woman and that she was too young to be that. She was okay with it at first; things went smoothly. But after too much time together, she started getting out of line, calling too much, stalking him, and doing things that would turn him off. When she told him that she was pregnant, he knew it was time to leave her alone. He would belittle her, yell at her, and mistreat her, but no matter what, she still wanted to be around him.

At first, he didn't believe that the kid was his. When Angel was born, there was no denying her. He told Teresa, "If my woman ever find out, I'm going to kill you." She agreed not to tell anyone who her baby's father was, and it went like that for years, until he became attracted to their daughter, Angel.

Albert had molested a few of his relatives in the past, but he had never gotten caught. He tried his hardest not to be attracted to her. She was his flesh and blood. There was just something about her that he couldn't shake. She was five or six when he started lusting over her and making inappropriate remarks to her. He had stopped when she turned eight, but he'd started something new with her when she was fourteen.

This was when he started really messing with her. She had developed breasts and a little booty to match.

One day she had come out in the front room with her tank top and pajama shorts on. She told her mother good night, and then she went back to her room. Albert watched as she swished down the hall, back to her room. Teresa caught him looking, but she didn't think anything of it.

After Teresa had given him some ass, he decided that he'd go check up on his daughter. To Teresa, this was the first time since Angel was born that he'd acted concerned about her. Teresa smiled after he told her that. In her head, she thought that she was finally getting the family she had always longed for.

When he walked into Angel's room, she was fast asleep in her twin bed. He closed the door behind him and walked over to her. She looked so beautiful and slept so peacefully. He kneeled down and pulled the covers off of her. Her titties were poking out of the tank, so he lifted it up and began fondling them.

She was sleeping so hard that she had no clue what was going on. He then decided to taste them, hoping they would taste better than her mother's. He placed one of her titties in his mouth and began flicking his tongue across her nipple. He placed his left hand in her panties and began playing with her pussy. He began to feel bad, and he quickly slid his hand out and pulled her shirt back down. He covered her up and left the room.

Teresa wondered what was taking him so long. When he returned, she asked, "What took you so long?" He told her that he was watching her sleep. That made Teresa smile again.

That was the first time he had touched his only child, but it was far from the last. Every time he came over, he made his way into Angel's room. He would touch her, suck her titties, and sometimes he would eat her pussy. She was a heavy sleeper, so she never had any idea that any of this was going on.

Teresa started to catch on and realized that he was not going in there to check up on Angel. One day she snuck behind him to see what he was really doing in there. When she cracked the door open and peeked in, she saw him with her daughter's legs wide open, his face in between. She watched with tears in her eyes as he sucked, slurped, and nibbled on his daughter's virgin pussy.

She tiptoed back to her room and cried. She couldn't believe it. She'd already had the feeling he was eyeballing Angel, but to actually see it was a different ball game. She hated Angel at this point. Up until then, the two of them had had a pretty good relationship, because they were all the other had. That relationship turned sour.

She started resenting having her daughter, since it was because of Angel that she had practically lost her man. She began being the meanest woman alive to Angel. Angel never knew why her mother started being cruel to her, but she did know that her mother strongly disliked her.

One day after school Angel was beyond tired and decided to rest up for later. She had plans to go to her friend Octavia's party, so the rest was needed. Albert had come over and had had Teresa suck his dick. Teresa was irritated by the fact that he didn't even want to fuck her after she was done.

He got up and headed to Angel's room. He closed and locked the door. He pulled the covers off of her and threw them on the floor. He pulled her bottoms down and began licking her pussy. After he felt it was wet enough, he slid his dick inside. He had never possessed a big dick, so it only made Angel jerk a little. She still remained sound asleep.

Being inside of her never-before-touched pussy, he reached ecstasy and came inside of her. He didn't think anything of it, because she wasn't having periods, to his knowledge. He slid her panties up, and she started moving, as if she was about to wake up. He quickly unlocked and opened the door. When she opened her eyes, he was leaving her room.

Angel had no idea why her dad had been in her room. But she wasn't even sure that he had actually been there, since she'd been half asleep the whole time. She sat up and saw her covers on the floor and knew something wasn't right. She just didn't know exactly what it was. Her mother knew what was going on. By this point, it had been going on for an entire year, and Teresa felt she had to accept it in order to get some of Albert's time.

Albert pulled up in front of Teresa's house and sighed. He hadn't seen her in years. He'd heard she'd been diagnosed with cancer and that she had recently passed out. They said somebody called the police from her house, but she was there alone when they arrived. He walked to the door and knocked firmly. Moments later, a fragile Teresa opened the door. She gave him an evil look, a look that simply said "What the fuck you want?"

He smiled. She wasn't the old scary-ass Teresa she used to be. She had grown some balls, because the old Teresa would have known better not to give him any look but a respectful one. To his surprise, she let him in. He noticed how bad she looked. She was skinny as a toothpick, and she was completely bald. He figured life was going to kill her, so he didn't need to.

They didn't say much. Actually, Teresa didn't say anything. He told her that he'd heard about her condition and wanted to check up on her. Teresa knew all too well what "check up on" meant in his vocabulary. She had a feeling he was looking for Angel. She didn't know where she was. If she did, she wouldn't have dared to tell him. He went on and on about how jail had changed him for the better, but she knew he was full of bullshit. Finally, the moment she had been waiting for came.

"So how's Angel?" he asked.

"She's good, I guess. I haven't talked to her. Why? You wanna go and fuck her like you used to?" she asked boldly, with disgust. She had held the hurt in for far too long, and now it was spilling over. She wanted to kill him for hurting her daughter. However, she figured life would get him.

Albert wanted to smack the shit out of Teresa for saying that. He wasn't thinking about fucking her. The only fuck he had in mind was fucking her up. "Teresa, don't start with me. I came here to get things straight," he lied.

She saw straight through the lies he told. He didn't give a fuck about them, and he showed it every chance he got. She figured enough was enough. It was clearly time for him to leave. She started cursing him out, and then she kicked him out. She didn't know why she had let him in to begin with.

He got up and left. On his way back to the car, he thought, *Maybe I should kill her.* He snapped out of it. Killing Angel would kill her. He got in the car and pulled off. He knew he had to teach Teresa a lesson, because she must've forgotten his capabilities.

Cliff was scared straight after watching that video. He was being beyond nice to Angel, hoping he didn't trigger that character she was when she was with Face. He apologized every day for beating her with the belt and just for putting his hands on her in general.

She didn't know where this sudden niceness was coming from, but she was going to take full advantage of it. She still had welts on her legs, which were healing slowly. Her mind was heavily on Crystal, and she believed that now was the time to go to Chicago to get her.

She didn't know how she would get it done, but she knew it had to be done soon. Since Cliff was trying to be so kind to her, she thought maybe he would let her have some space out of his sight. She decided she would tell him that she was going to the mall. She would use whatever money he gave her and put it with the money she had gotten from Omar and use it to get her sister. She already had the money from Omar and her purse ready for her departure. She had already called the airport and knew that a flight would be leaving in three hours. She had to move fast.

On her way down the stairs, she met Cliff, who was coming up. "Hey, baby," Angel said. She stopped in front of him, and he stopped.

"Yeah?" Cliff responded nervously. He didn't know what she wanted. All he knew was that he was not fucking her. He saw what sex made her do, and he had no time to fall victim.

"I need to go to the mall," she said, placing her hand on his shoulder.

He went in his pocket and gave her the keys to his Benz and his black card. She took them and moved out of his way. She didn't think it would be this easy, but she was glad it was. Cliff was glad it went smoothly too. He was happy that she didn't want anything too big. At this point, Angel could have said she wanted everything he had, and he would have given it to her. He went upstairs, embarrassed that this girl had him in fear.

Angel jetted out the door and headed to the platinum-colored Benz. Trist was pulling in. She hadn't seen him or talked to him since Miami. She figured that he must've stayed there with some girl he was dealing with. Angel had caught a feeling about that. She didn't have shit to say to him, so she slammed the car door shut and started the ignition.

She was on a mission, and Trist was not it. While driving down to the airport, she began to wonder why she was feeling him so much. He was a no-good nigga. Maybe it was the dick that had her checking for him. She wasn't sure. He made her feel good, and in her lifetime, only one other person had done that for her. That was Omar. She decided she needed to be in Chicago. She needed to get her sister and her man back.

When I arrived in Chicago, I wondered how this would go. I didn't know if I would make it to my sister or if the Feds would get to me first. I had to try my luck, either way it went. I had no bags, only my purse. I knew I would have to buy everything I needed for my stay here. I went to the front desk to rent a car.

While in Atlanta, I had gotten myself a new identity for my new look. The lady smiled at me and told me what my car choices were. I decided just to take the Nissan Altima. She told me to wait out front and an employee would drive it to the door for me. There were a lot of people, both male and female, staring at my ass. I didn't care as long as they weren't staring at my face. I walked outside and waited for the Nissan. When it finally pulled up, the employee got out and stood there staring.

"Is this for Crystal?" I asked.

He was still, like he had seen a ghost. "Y-y-yeah," he finally answered as he extended his arm to hand me the keys. I grabbed them and walked over to the driver's side. I didn't know what had him frozen, but whatever it was, I had no time to figure it out.

I headed to the last place that I'd called home before I fled to Atlanta, Omar's house. I didn't know if he had moved on or if things were still the same, but it would be worth a try. His Charger was in front of the house, so I knew he was home. I prayed he didn't have a new girl. I wouldn't be able to handle that heartbreak.

I parked my car behind his and turned it off. I sat in the car for a minute, deciding if this was the smart thing to do. I was here now, so why

not? I got out of the car and looked myself over.
I was wearing some skinny jeans and an orange
baby doll shirt that flared at the bottom. I had
some leopard pumps on and carried a brown
Gucci purse. I felt cute.

I slowly walked up to his door. I sighed before
I knocked. All I could do was hope for the best.
He came to the door without a shirt on his back.
His tattoo-covered body looked sexy. I smiled.

"Can I help you?" he asked.

"Can I come in?" I asked as I peeked into his
house.

"Huh?" he answered. I had totally forgotten
that I had had the surgery done and I didn't look
the same anymore

"It's me. Angel," I said, hoping that he cared
and the feelings were still there. He looked at me
for a good minute before he responded.

"Angel," he repeated.

I nodded my head.

He grabbed me and hugged me so tight that I
could barely breathe. He moved out of the way and
let me in. He closed the door behind us, and I went
straight to the couch. We had a lot of catching up to
do. He sat next to me. His body was close to mine,
and it made me wet.

"You were at KOD Urban Week," he said while
pointing his finger at me. I was ashamed, but I
admitted it.

"You had Luxury all in ya' damn face too," I said, deciding to throw that in there.

"She's a stripper, and it's a strip club. I don't want that ho," he assured me. "All I want is you." He softly kissed me on my lips. I felt my juices start to flow more. I hadn't had a piece of dick since Face, and that was way too long ago. I was yearning for it, and being that I missed him and he missed me, I knew this was going to be epic.

He picked me up and carried me up the stairs. It felt so good to be in his arms. It felt like home. He laid me down on the bed and unbuckled my pants. I lifted my ass and pulled my pants and panties down. I kicked off my pumps, and then I pulled my pants and panties from around my legs. He put his head between my legs and spread my pussy lips. He hadn't even started eating me out and my body was already tingling.

I was ready.

He twirled his tongue in circles on my clit. I arched my back and held on to the headboard. He started nibbling on it and then sucking on it gently. I wanted to cry. It felt so good, and I wanted more. My legs started to close, and I inched to the top of the bed. He grabbed my legs tighter and lifted his head.

"Where you going?" he asked, looking sexy.

I smiled and shook my head. He then crawled his way up and slid his long, thick dick inside of me. This was the moment that I had been waiting for. He twirled his dick in a circular motion inside of me as I grabbed his back and stuck my nails in it. It felt so good. He lay down on me and grabbed my shoulders to help him bounce me on his dick better. I moaned and pulled him closer to me to get his dick farther inside.

"I missed you," he whispered in my ear.

"I missed you more," I moaned.

I really did miss him, but this moment was worth the wait. He lifted my leg up in the air and flipped me over, placing me in the doggy-style position. I lifted myself up and arched my back to serve him better. He started humping me slowly and then sped up. I threw it back at him, and then he stopped and let me do all the work. He sat on his knees, and I bounced on his dick. I had a flashback of Mike and Nicole at the airport. I became pissed all over again. I thrust hard and fast, mad at the world.

"Baby, baby, it's so good," Omar moaned.

I stopped humping and started grinding. I cupped my titties, giving it to him good. When Mike found out that I had fucked another man, he would be pissed. He deserved to be mad. *Fuck him,* I thought as Omar came inside of me.

He held me tight and continued whispering "I love you" in my ear. As we lay down, both of our bodies dripped sweat. I was tired, and I was sure he was too. We fell asleep in no time.

When I woke up, it was dark outside and Omar was nowhere to be found. I looked at my phone, which was on vibrate. I saw that Cliff had been blowing my phone up. I took the battery out and put both the battery and my phone back in my purse.

Omar came into the room.

"Where were you, baby?" I asked as I stood up to hug him.

He smiled. "You act like we didn't just get done fucking."

We both decided take a shower. We washed each other's bodies off, and when we were done, we dried each other off. Later he cooked spaghetti and fish for us, and we sat at the table with candles lit between us.

"So what made you come back?" Omar asked. He was free balling in his all-black basketball shorts.

"My little sister," I answered.

"You got a sister?" he asked, as if he didn't know that already.

"Yeah. Didn't you meet her before?" I asked him. I was almost certain that she had let him in my house before.

He shook his head no, which left me confused.

"Well, after I get her, you guys are going to have to meet."

He asked me what life was like in Atlanta, and I began telling him about my bittersweet life with Cliff. He told me that he had gotten a girlfriend, but she was in New York for her family reunion. That spoiled my appetite.

"Do you love her?" I asked, praying that he didn't.

He shook his head yeah. I could've cried. I had pictured that we would be together in the long run. What was I thinking when I believed he would wait for me? I was gone only three months, and he was already with someone new.

He told me that they already had relations before I left. Once I left, he told me they had gotten closer. I just sat and smiled, like I was happy for him, when in reality I was sick to my stomach. I wanted Omar for myself, and I strongly believed we were meant to be.

Home wasn't so sweet, after all.

Chapter 19

I decided that being under Omar, knowing that his heart was with someone else, was not a smart choice. I figured I would spend only one night at his house and the rest at a hotel. My feet rested in his lap as we sat on the couch, talking. I was telling him about Cliff and how abusive he was to me.

"Word. You ain't know about him beating his old girlfriend?" he asked.

I shook my head no. "I mean, not previously. I didn't know until we were already. By then, it was too late," I explained. Personally, I had never heard of the man until I had met him at the law firm.

"Yeah, Beautyful, the stripper that be with Luxury, was his old girl, but now she turned out," he said.

I sat there in a daze. I didn't even know that they used to be together. They had never talked about it or given me the impression that they had a past. Then I remembered her encouraging me to leave him alone.

It was a small world.

"Yeah, his brother, Tristan, had a thing for me too, which made Cliff watch *me* like a hawk instead of his brother."

"He got a brother?" he asked.

"Yeah. Well, at least he said that was his brother," I replied, unsure at this point.

"Naw, that nigga ain't got no brother. That's my favorite boxer. I would know," he said as he rubbed my feet. "As a matter of fact, I don't even know of him hanging with a nigga by that name."

It was like he was accusing me of lying about Trist. What would be my reason for lying about his existence? I hated more than anything to be called a liar indirectly, so I instantly got pissed. I moved my legs from his lap and placed my feet on the floor. I crossed my arms and rolled my eyes. I was ready to go. It was a new day, and it was the day to go and get my little sister.

First, I needed to get some clothes. I told Omar that I would be back. I had to go shopping. To my surprise, he wanted to accompany me. I didn't really want him tagging along, but I wasn't going to be cruel and tell him no. I decided, since he was joining, he would be paying.

We headed to Chicago Premium Outlets I just needed something to put on for that day. I would worry about the rest of the days as they came about. After he bought me all the things I needed for the day, we went back to his house so that I could shower and get dressed.

Done with my hot shower, I walked out of the bathroom with my towel wrapped around me. Omar stood up and looked at my legs.

"What happened?" he asked.

I walked past him and sat on the bed. I wasn't in the mood for him to feel sorry for me. I didn't need the pity. I continued to dry off in silence. Omar sat next to me and watched me. My legs still looked pretty bad, but they were healing. Welts covered the majority of my legs, and they were dark marks, too. They were very noticeable.

"You need to leave him, Angel," he warned, as if I wasn't aware.

I turned to him. "I know that, Omar. It's just right now he's all I have to get by." I was praying he'd understand, but at the same time I didn't need his understanding. He was involved with someone else, and I didn't matter to him any longer.

"You can get by. You don't need him," he said.

I wished those statements were true, but deep inside, I knew they weren't. I had no job and little money. Now that I was bringing my sister along with me, I needed some guaranteed money. Everything needed to be guaranteed because she depended on me.

"Angel, I really wish that me and you could have turned out a lot differently," he said as he wrapped his arm around my waist. I rested my head on his shoulder. I wished the same, but that was wishful thinking. It was too late now.

I stood up to put my clothes on, and after I was done with that, I was out the door. I told Omar that I was going to visit my mom and that I wanted to go alone. He nodded his head as if he understood. He told me to promise that I'd come back. I did, highly doubting that I would.

For some odd reason, I wanted to drive past my mother's house. After I did, I circled the house, stopped, and put my car in park. I sat in front of her house and cried. I sat and reminisced about how things were before I became a teenager and how they suddenly changed when I became one. We used to be like best friends.

I had always said we never had that bond, but we did. When it faded away, it felt like it had never existed. She was coldhearted toward me. She was very manipulative. She just didn't care for me anymore. Tears rolled down my face as I reflected on the day I came back and how she looked. She was thin and sickly. I finally felt as though she cared. Finally, I mattered, and then she was gone. I took my car out of park and headed across town to Tiffany's house.

When I arrived at Tiffany's, her kids were in the front yard, running around. There was no sign of Crystal. *Maybe she's in the house and doesn't want to come out and play.* She never was a fan of the sun. I walked up to the door and knocked loudly. Her door was open, but she kept the outside out with her screen door.

Tiffany came to the door with a look of worry on her face. She looked the same as she did when we used to hang together. She was holding a baby who appeared to be six or seven months old.

"Yes?" she asked.

"It's me, Angel," I said, realizing she didn't know who I was because of the surgery.

"Angel," she said in shock.

"Yes. Angel," I repeated.

Her eyes got big, and she shut her door in my face. I was baffled. What was wrong with her? I knocked on the door again.

She opened it and said, "You're wanted for murder, Angel."

"I know that, but I came to get Crystal." For some odd reason I felt like she was trying to keep me from my sister.

"Angel, there is no Crystal here."

"What?"

"You've been calling and asking me about her, and I don't know her. Honey, I don't have her," she said calmly.

She must have been mistaken, because she came to pick Crystal up from my house the day I fled town. I reminded her of that.

"No, Angel. I didn't. The only Crystal I know is you." She was still talking very calmly. "Remember when we were younger, your mom used to always call you by your middle name, Crystal," she said, trying to refresh my memory.

I stood there looking dumbfounded. I really couldn't remember my childhood, other than the way my mother treated me. She told me that I needed to go seek some help and take my medication. She also told me that I wasn't safe in Chicago.

I told her, "Thank you." Then I left her premises. Before pulling off, I sat in front of her house in my car in deep thought.

How could she tell me that my sister didn't exist? I had raised her for the past three years. I knew I wasn't imagining her. I couldn't be. The only person that could tell me anything I needed to know about my life was my mother, but she was gone.

Crystal does exist, Angel, I thought to myself. I decided to ride past my mother's house one last time. I needed to sit and think about where my sister could be. I assumed that she missed me and had run away and that Tiffany had played the "Angel is crazy" card on me because she felt bad.

I parked my car in front of my mother's house and cut off the engine. I sat there gazing out of my car door window, daydreaming. Someone knocked on my window. I jumped and looked. I was startled.

It was my mom. Now I knew I was crazy. She was dead . . . or was she? She was looking hard in the window. I figured she was trying to figure out who was parked in front of her house.

"Let down the damn window, " she said.

I started the car and lowered the window hesitantly.

"What are you doing here? Who you looking for, lady?" she asked me.

"Mom? I thought you were dead," I cried.

"Mom?" she asked, with a puzzled look on her face. She stared at me for what seemed like forever. "Crystal?" she said, not really sure.

I was still in awe, trying to figure out if this really was my mom who stood before me or if I was having another one of my episodes. I told her that I came back for Crystal. She gave me this pitiful look that said she felt sorry for me.

"Baby, you really need your meds." Tears formed in her eyes. She opened the passenger door and told me to come in her house. I cut the car off once again and followed her inside her house. I sat down on the couch, and my mother sat down next to me.

"Listen, baby. There is no Crystal," she told me sadly.

I stared at her bony face, not believing a word she said. "How can you deny your own child?" I responded. My mother hadn't changed a bit.

"Listen, if you were taking your medicine like you were supposed to, you would know that Crystal is not your little sister. Your name is Crystal. Angel Crystal Jacobs."

It made perfect sense, but I knew that I had a sister and that I took care of her.

"After you, I couldn't have any more kids," she explained, moving closer to me. "You're not even stable enough to look after a kid."

Tears slowly fell from her eyes, and I knew she was hurt to see me like this.

"Mom, I know Crystal exists. How dare you call me a liar!"

"Angel, as hard as it is for me to be the one to tell you that Crystal is just a character you made up to run away from the bad things you were actually experiencing, I want you to face your problems. Baby, there is no little sister named Crystal."

I still wasn't convinced. I still wanted to believe she was lying.

She placed her hand on my thigh and began pouring her heart out.

"Look, we've been at it for far too long. My days are coming to an end, and I don't wanna die knowing that I left you confused and alone." Tears welled up in her eyes, which made me cry even harder. "You were my only child, and I loved you more than I loved myself. Your father used to go in your room and molest you. Then, shortly after he started that, you smoked some bad weed and was diagnosed with bipolar disorder."

She wiped her eyes and took a deep breath.

My mind was racing as I recalled smoking with Davon at a party.

"You were dating that boy Mike, and that's all you remember. Whenever you would have a breakdown, you'd always mention his name. You blame him for you losing your baby because you thought he was the father, but he wasn't." She paused

I could tell whatever she was about to say was probably the hardest thing she would ever say.

"What do you mean, it wasn't Mike's?" I questioned while standing up. It had always been Mike's, and I was beyond tired of Mike being excused.

"It was Albert's," she confessed, looking up at me. She put her face in her hands and began crying hysterically.

It was like at that moment the world stopped turning and was caving in on me. "It was Albert's" echoed in my brain, and her telling me my father raped me and his name was Albert let me know it was him. He was my child's father and I was so disgusted. I wanted to rip my heart out and die right there. How could he?

Memories of me waking up to find him leaving my room played in my mind. I cried my soul out as I recalled the many times I would pretend I was asleep just so I wouldn't have to confront him raping me. I had pushed those nightmares to the back of my head for so long that to me they no longer exist. I'd pinned them on Crystal, because she deserved to be hurt more than I did.

Why Tiffany had told me she never had my sister and why Omar had said he' d never met her now made sense.

I was her.

I was Crystal. I was living out my childhood, but I was on the outside, looking in. Things that had happened throughout my life, I made them happen in Crystal's life. I was in denial. I was the one my daddy had raped. I was the one whom my mother had made act dumb when they were running studies on me.

I was the one who had gone to the school where you had to physically go and get the child out of class. And I was the one who everyone thought had a problem. I cried my eyes out on my mother's shoulder.

She rubbed my hair and told me everything would be okay. For once, I believed her. I couldn't believe that I had actually thought that I had a little sister. I'd really thought that I was taking care of her and that I saw her. Everything felt so real, but how?

I had a problem, and now I was finally admitting it.

Chapter 20

Cliff was beyond pissed that Angel hadn't returned with his car or his black card. He was even more irritated at the fact that she hadn't returned at all. It had been almost two days since he had seen her, and he was worried that maybe she was in jail. He decided to call booking to see if she'd been incarcerated.

When he called, the operator told him that they didn't have a Crystal Jacobs or an Angel Jacobs. Now he was sure that she had run off with his shit. He decided to ask Chelsea if she had heard from her. When Chelsea said no, his suspicions were confirmed. He wondered whom she had run off with. He called her a million times, and she never answered a phone call. He left voice messages and sent text messages, but to no avail.

He needed to know where she was. She was his fifty-thousand-dollar ticket. He couldn't let that get away, and since he hadn't got any fights in the past month or so, that money was needed. His phone danced on the table while singing "Making Love to the Money" by Gucci Mane.

He looked at the screen to see who was calling. It was Porsha.

"What's up?" he answered.

"Where's Angel? Albert is out and ready for her," she said.

He hated to be the bearer of bad news, but he had no clue and that was what he told her.

She was pissed. She had given him the easiest assignment in the world, and he couldn't even fulfill it. "What do you mean, you don't know?" she asked with an attitude.

"Exactly what I said! *I don't* know," he replied.

She smacked her lips and hung up on him. Cliff felt that whether he had Angel or not, they still owed him some type of money. He had kept her out of jail for months and for that, they owed him at least half the money.

He called Porsha back. She answered with the same attitude she'd hung up with.

"Listen, lose the damn attitude, 'cause whether we find her or not, he ain't marrying yo' dumb ass. Now, what I'm calling for is I feel I deserve half of that money because I kept her out of jail," he said, knowing she would agree.

She chuckled and politely said, "Nigga, you ain't getting shit." Then, once again, she hung up in Cliff's face.

He heard complete silence, so he looked at his phone. It was lit up, and the screen read CALL ENDED. In Cliff's head, Porsha was playing with fire now, and she was about to get burned.

Two could play that game, but Clifton Moore played it better.

Albert stayed away from Porsha as much as possible. He always had her car which helped him stay out of her sight. He was riding by the park, where a few young cats were playing basketball, when he spotted a pretty young thing. She was thick, and her hair weave was fresh. She was getting out of a brand-new Nissan Altima.

He slowed down and crept behind her, watching her walk over to the basketball court. She looked behind her and saw a car, so she moved out of the way. Albert slowed down some more and drove at the same pace at which she was walking. When he got to her side, she looked at him and frowned.

He chuckled. Young girls were good at catching attitudes for no reason. Her eyes seemed familiar, but he couldn't recall where he'd seen them.

She looked like the type who liked niggas in the streets. Maybe she was one of those girls that visited one of the inmates while he was in jail.

He had it etched in his head that he was going to get her or at least fuck her. She was way too thick and cute not to. He pulled Porsha's car over and got out. The thick chick was a great distance away by this point, so Albert had to jog to get to where she was.

"Hey!" He was rocking some basketball gym shorts and a wife beater. His muscular frame and jail tattoos made him look younger than he was. Porsha had just purchased him some all-white shell-toe Adidas, so in Albert's head, he was looking young and fly.

The thick chick stopped and turned around in Albert's direction. Her tight purple miniskirt and matching camisole looked like they'd been painted on her. Her stomach was as flat as a board, and her ass and titties were voluptuous. Not to mention her skinny waist and wide hips. She was a perfect ten to him.

"Yes?" she asked.

He smiled as he walked over to her and then stopped when they were within arms' reach.

"What's your name, gorgeous?" he asked. He was an old head, so he knew that younger girls liked when a nigga came at them politely.

She scrunched up her face. She wasn't the least bit interested, but she still answered his question. "Crystal," she said softly. "Yours?"

As soon as the words escaped her mouth, she wished she'd told him that her name was Angel, but now it was too late.

"I'm Chris," he said, smiling. "Crystal and Chris." He chuckled.

She smiled at the fact that they had similar names.

"Well, it was nice meeting you," he said, extending his hand. She put her hand out to shake his. He grabbed it and kissed it. "Take care," he said and left her standing there.

She was impressed. She had never had a nigga stop her just to find out her name. Most niggas wanted her number, and they all wanted her body. She turned back around and began walking to the basketball court to watch the guys play.

Albert jumped back in the car and headed to pick Porsha up from work. He knew in due time that the thick chick would be trying to find him. She was curious, and curiosity always killed the cat. He had plans on getting her cat.

When he pulled up into Bennifeld law firm's parking lot, he noticed Porsha standing alone with her arms crossed. It was obvious that he was running late and she was very upset. She got in the car and was getting ready to start an argument, but after Albert rubbed her inner thigh and got her soaking wet, she changed her mind.

He continued rubbing her thigh as they cruised through the streets of Chicago. He was wondering where Angel was. He had let her live long enough.

"So what's the word on Angel?" he asked.

Porsha was dreading answering this question. She knew she was supposed to be on top of this situation, but there was nothing she could really do about it. "Well, Cliff . . ." she began.

Albert already knew where this was headed, straight into an excuse. "Look, save the damn lies and shit, and tell me what the fuck is up." He grew angry. He knew her dumb ass would fuck this up for him. She didn't know that Angel was the only reason he was involved with her.

Her smile quickly became a frown, which drifted into tears. She just wanted him to love her. She could see right through this situation. Albert didn't give a fuck about her, and that hurt the most. *What will it take for him to realize I'm the one for him?* she thought.

Albert was irritated at the fact that she was useless. He pulled up to the Lake Meadows, where her apartment was located, and parked. She looked at him with evil eyes and mumbled

something he didn't catch. He didn't say anything, and she knew how he truly felt without
him saying a word

She smacked her lips and opened her door.
She looked at him one last time and said, "Self-
ish-ass bitch! I see where Angel gets it from,"
and then she slammed the door. Albert chuckled.
He knew she was just upset that things weren't
going the way she'd envisioned. Then again, it
wasn't going how he'd planned either.

Porsha went up to her one-bedroom apartment
and flopped down on the couch. She should have
known that he wasn't shit. Hell, his daughter
wasn't shit, either. She was tired of niggas trying
to get over on her. She was a queen and deserved to
be treated like one. She had something that she
knew would set his ass straight forever.

Mama had always said, "You play with fire,
you will get burned." She was going to make sure
that Albert would feel the wrath. Even though
she never liked Angel, she'd grown to stand her.
For that reason, she would do her a favor and
send her father away forever.

She picked up her cell phone and dialed three
numbers. She wanted to press SEND, but then she
second-guessed her decision. Was she making
the right choice, or was it going to backfire in her
face and haunt her forever? She was in what she
thought was love, but love didn't love her.

"Press SEND or END, Porsha, damn!" she yelled at herself while her cell phone rattled in her hand from her nervousness. Someone had to lose in this game, and it for damn sure wasn't going to be her.

I was lying in my hotel room with a headache that made my head tremble. This hangover was killing me. I had gone to Vision Nightclub to get a few drinks that I damn for sure needed. After my long conversation with my mother and after Omar telling me he had a girl, I was stressed. I sat up in the bed, and my head instantly spun.

I placed my hand on my forehead and closed my eyes. I inched my way out of the bed to get my purse, which sat beside a pile of dirty clothes. I grabbed my brown Gucci bag and dug inside for my BlackBerry and its battery. I put the battery inside my phone and cut it on.

I had so many voice mails, it was ridiculous. The majority of them were from Cliff and Omar. Cliff was going on and on about how he had trusted me and I had betrayed him. He wasn't as angry as I expected him to be, but I could tell he was mad, though. Omar was telling me he missed me and asking me to answer so that he could tell me something. I didn't really care to know what it was he had to tell me. As far as I knew, he was already spoken for.

My mother was also one of the people who left me messages. She simply said that I was heavily on her mind and she didn't know if that was a good or bad thing. I decided not to call her back. She always seemed to bring tears to my eyes. I decided to call Cliff. It wasn't like he could do anything to me, anyway. I was clear across the map, and he had no clue where to find me. I didn't even think his phone rang before he answered it.

"Angel, where are you?" he asked with a calm voice.

"Chicago. Your car is at the airport, and it's available for you to get. The keys are there, and your black card is in the glove compartment." That was all I had of his, so I figured he'd be satisfied.

"That's not the issue, Angel," he responded. I didn't understand why there was even an issue to begin with. It was clear. We weren't in love, and what we'd had was just a convenience for both of us.

"Look, I'm not what you want. I fucked your brother, Trist, and I fucked Face. I'm a ho. I was stripping at KOD, and I just fucked my ex all of two days ago." I needed to get it off my chest.

He sat there, silent, and then he said, "Angel, I don't have a brother, nor do I know a Trist."

I looked around my room. I didn't know why, but when he said that, all of a sudden I felt like somebody was watching me. Omar had said that Cliff had only a sister. If Cliff didn't know Trist, how did I meet him at his house?

"What?" I was confused, because I knew Trist existed.

"I don't have a brother. Who is Trist?" he asked.

I hung up the phone. I leaned back and looked up to the ceiling, and it appeared to be moving in a circular motion. "I really am crazy," I said out loud. "I'm fucking nuts!" I laughed.

I began laughing so hard that tears started to fall from my eyes. I guess I was a little off my rocker, but who gave a damn? I decided that I needed to go find me something to wear for the day. Despite my hangover, I managed to get up and take a shower. I threw on the T-shirt and shorts that I had previously worn, and then I headed out the door.

I went to the mall ended up buying a few PINK sweat suits from Victoria's Secret. I changed into one in the dressing room after I paid for them and went about my day. My stomach was growling, so I headed to McDonald's. I decided to dine in, being that I had nowhere to be.

I sat there and daydreamed about that strong, muscular man that I had run into at the park. He was handsome and looked familiar, but I couldn't put my finger on where I had seen him before. He had me wanting more. Maybe it was the way he approached me, or was it how he left me there in awe? I was in a daze as I looked out the window, until someone sat down and blocked my view. It was him.

"Hey, beautiful," he said with a smile full of pearly whites. I instantly snapped out of my trance. I smiled shyly.

"Hey, you," I said softly.

"I been looking for you," he declared.

He had been heavily on my mind since the first day we met. I was happy that we were finally meeting again. There were a few things I wanted to do to him. His creatively tattooed arms were exposed, and from the way they looked, I knew he had gotten them done in jail. I loved me a thug, and he was just that. I could tell.

"Let's go somewhere better to get something to eat. You're worth more than the dollar menu," he told me.

I looked down at my untouched nuggets and fries and took him up on his offer. We ended up at a semi-expensive restaurant. As we sat there talking, I visualized us in bed. I kept trying to tell myself to keep it classy. In my mind, I kept it nasty.

After we ate, he excused himself and went to the bathroom. I sat alone at the table, looking at my silverware. There was something about the steak knife that made me want it for myself, so I quickly wrapped it up in my napkin and placed it in my purse. When he came back, he put money, including a nice tip, on the table and we headed out.

He asked me if he could take me to a hotel, and I didn't tell him no. I left my car at the restaurant, and we left in his Honda. I remembered Porsha's ass having a car identical to this one. I kind of wondered if she still had it.

We pulled up to Hotel Sax on Dearborn Street. We parked the car and headed inside. I sat down on the sofa that was in the lobby while he got the room. After he got the key, we went straight to the elevator. We stepped in, he pressed five, and the elevator doors closed.

Porsha had to do it. It was killing her inside not to. She had a gut feeling that he was some- where fucking another bitch. She couldn't have that. She pressed SEND. The operator quickly got on the line.

"Nine-one-one. What's the emergency?" she asked.

"Yes, there's a guy I know who is plotting to kill his daughter," Porsha said, quickly regretting it.

"And how do you know this, ma'am?"

"He wanted my friend Cliff to help him set her up, but I just can't let them, and I want to help before he kills her," Porsha cried. She felt bad for Angel all of a sudden and knew that Albert was going to get her if he ever caught up with her. She told the operator everything she needed to know, except for her involvement in the whole ordeal.

When she got off of the phone with the police, she felt that a weight had lifted from her shoulders. She felt that she had done a good deed. She wished that she could call and warn Angel personally. She still had her number, but she figured she had gotten it changed. She thought about sending her a picture of Albert with a text that said, Stay away.

Porsha got up to clear her house of Albert. She decided she would pack up all his shit and have it sitting in the hallway when he got back. She was tired of being played for a fool. He was too damn old to be trying to be a player. She headed into her confined bedroom and went over to the closet, forcefully opening it. She snatched his shit off the hangers and threw it onto the floor. He had only about ten outfits. She took his shoes from the bottom of the closet and threw them on top of the pile she'd started for him.

At this point, she was dripping with sweat and tears. She wiped her forehead and headed over to the nightstand, where more of his underclothes were stored. She pulled the two drawers completely out and launched them across the room, one by one. One of the drawers put a hole in the wall.

She dropped to her knees and cried. She was tired of the same shit over and over again. She lay down on top of his clothes and wept. After about ten minutes, too long, she got up and headed to the kitchen to get a garbage bag. He was garbage, and his shit deserved to be treated as such.

Her face was full of tears, and her mind was filled with unresolved issues. She stood in her bedroom doorway with the black Hefty trash bag in her hand. She stared at all his shit piled up in the middle of her bedroom floor. Then it dawned on her, she'd paid for that shit. That nigga wasn't getting shit.

She hoped and prayed that he got the death penalty for trying to kill his own flesh and blood. She slid down the door frame and sat on the floor. She had never questioned why he wanted

Angel out of the game so bad. He'd said only that she had accused him of raping her, so why would they prosecute him if they never proved it?

Albert was a fucking pedophile. She shook her head in disgust and decided to call Kim. They hadn't talked since Albert was released, so they had a lot of catching up to do. She dialed Kim's number and waited for her to answer.

Albert was shocked that Crystal was willing to go to a hotel with him. He guessed she was on the same thing as he was, fucking. He didn't want her as his woman, and she didn't want him as her man; they just wanted to enjoy this moment.

She was probably the sexiest girl he had ever seen. He opened the door for them and let her walk in first. She smiled. He knew young niggas never did that for their women. He had asked the receptionist to bring some alcoholic beverages up to their room. The drunker they were, the freakier they'd be.

She flopped down on the bed, on her stomach, and her ass jiggled. Albert licked his lips as he watched. You could tell she didn't have any panties on. She flipped over on her back and smiled again.

He headed over to sit next to her, but the knocks at the door interrupted him. He turned around to answer it. He knew it was room service. The nerdy hotel employee that resembled Harry Potter had a bottle of champagne and a bucket of ice in his hands. Albert grabbed them from the Harry Potter look-alike and tipped him.

He closed the door and retrieved two glasses for the two of them. He had his back toward her as he poured the drinks. When he turned back around, he saw her rolling up a blunt. The smell that lingered in the room let him know she was smoking what he called Loud. It was called Loud because it was a smell you couldn't ignore.

"You smoke?" she asked while licking the blunt to seal the deal.

He nodded his head yeah, even though he didn't. He figured he needed a high to keep up with her young, thick ass. She flicked her lighter across the blunt to make sure that it stayed wrapped, and then she sparked it. She inhaled the blunt, and then she exhaled. The smoke came out of her mouth, and then she sucked it back in, and then it came out her nose.

"You smoke all the time?" he asked. In his eyes, she handled the weed like a nigga.

"Naw, I haven't smoked in years," she confessed as she flicked the ashes to the floor. She passed the blunt to him, and he hit it twice and passed it back. He was never a smoker, though he had done it here and there in the past.

He was ready to get the show on the road, and she could sense his impatience. She put her blunt out, and he handed her a glass of champagne. She downed three glasses, and he drank two. He could see she was going through some things just by the look on her face.

He lay down on the bed and pulled his dick out. He figured his sex could ease her mind, or maybe she could ease his. He was still annoyed at the fact that things weren't going as planned. How badly he wanted to kill Angel was sickening. If he could just cross paths with her, the rest would be history.

Crystal slid closer to him and grabbed his dick. She massaged his rock-solid dick, staring into his eyes the whole time. She was so familiar. Those eyes were too familiar. Had he already fucked her and couldn't remember? She looked no older than twenty-five.

"Condom?" she asked.

Albert pulled the condom out of his shoe and handed it to her. He had started storing them in his shoe because every time he came home, Porsha ransacked his pockets. She ripped it open and slid it down his shaft.

"You sure you ready?" she leaned in and asked. She licked his earlobe, and that gave him a tingly feeling.

"Of course," he answered.

She grabbed his face and began kissing him roughly. She stuck her tongue in his mouth and twirled it all around. She stood up and pulled her sweatpants down, and as he'd suspected, she didn't have on any panties. She pushed Albert back so that he would be lying flat on his back. Then she straddled him.

Omar sat on his bed, gazing at the ceiling. He had Angel heavily on his mind. Although his girl was lying right next to him, she couldn't stop him from thinking about Angel. He looked over at Kim and wished it was Angel. Kim was cute and all, but now that he thought about it, she was too damn loud.

He had met her at Bennifeld's when he had caught a little drug case. She was persistent about exchanging numbers, and they ended up doing so. Her sex and head game were worth every penny he spent on her, but she wasn't worth shit. He had gotten deeply involved with her after Angel had left.

Kim knew all about Angel, and it seemed as if that made her want him even more. Kim was just there to fill the void that Angel left. At first it had worked, but now that Angel was back in town, she was the one that he really wanted.

Kim's phone was ringing, so she moved to retrieve it from the nightstand. Omar snapped out of his trance. By how loud she was talking, he knew it was Porsha's lonely ass on the other line. Kim was telling her how the family reunion had gone and how she missed her. Her tone suddenly changed, and Omar knew something was wrong. Kim told Porsha that she was on her way, and then she hung up. She looked over at Omar and smiled.

"You know I love you, baby," she said seductively.

"Yeah, I know," Omar proclaimed. He wasn't so sure that he loved her too, so he didn't say it back.

She got down to where his dick was and pulled it out of his boxers. She began sucking his dick the way she had the first day they met. Although it felt good, he imagined that she was Angel. As he gripped her by the hair and let out low moans, he thought about all the times he fucked Angel. It was like heaven being inside of her, and he wanted that feeling again. Kim was slurping now, practically gargling on his dick. He bit his bottom lip.

It took no time for him to get close to reaching his peak. As he reached his finish line, he let out a loud moan and then declared, "I love you, Angel."

It seemed like at that moment the world stopped turning. Kim came up from down below and smacked the taste out of Omar's mouth. He didn't say or do anything. He knew he deserved every bit of that. Kim got up from out of the bed, mumbling a bunch of nothing. Omar never did get the opportunity to cum, but he did get close to Angel in that moment, so he was cool. He turned over on his side and proceeded to go to sleep.

Kim hopped back on the phone with Porsha, as loud as could be.

"Girl, why this nigga just call me Angel, though?" she complained as soon as Porsha answered. "Yeah, girl! I'm giving him the head like none other, and his dusty, broke ass calling me that nothing-ass bitch name. Did he forget *she* left *his* ass? I hope and pray Albert kill that ho, and then we'll see whose name he'll be screaming."

That was all Omar heard, and quite frankly, that was all he needed to hear.

Somebody was trying to kill the love of his life, and he had to do something. He decided to wait until Kim left to call Angel so that he could warn her. Kim left the house shortly after to tend to her lonely friend and to bitch about what had just taken place. When she was out of sight, Omar quickly dialed Angel's number. She never answered, so he decided to shoot her a text. He quickly wrote her something short and to the point.

I was just about to get in motion on Chris when my phone refused to shut up. I got up to put it on silent, but now I became a little worried. **Baby, some nigga named Albert is looking for you to kill you,** the text from Omar read. The only Albert I knew that would want to harm me was my dad.

I didn't know him from Adam and Eve, and so if I saw him, I wouldn't know him. I put the phone on silent and then placed it back in my purse. I decided to finish what I had started. I got on top of Chris and began bouncing up and down like a basketball.

He was gripping my ass so rough that I just knew my skin was going to break from his nails. He was talking kind of dirty, and I just tuned him out. I wanted to give him the kind of pussy his girl wished she could supply him with. I put my arm behind me and began playing with his balls.

"Crystal, baby," he moaned.

I sped up the ride. He had his eyes closed tight, but not as tight as my pussy. His long, thick dick overflowed my pussy. It wasn't a smooth ride at all. In fact, it kind of hurt, but I knew after a while I would master him. When it finally started to feel good, I slowed down the ride. I started to grind on him and twirl my body around. He moaned and groaned. His eyes remained shut the entire time.

Then that face popped up, and I grew scared. It was Mike. My eyes got so big, and I knew I had only so long to take care of this situation, and then the face went back to Chris's. I started breathing heavily. This hadn't happened in so long. I turned around, while keeping his dick inside of me, and kept popping on his dick. He was mumbling something that I could barely understand. He just wouldn't shut up, and he said something that made my skin crawl.

"That's right, Angel. Fuck Daddy the way ya' Mama couldn't."

The room started spinning, and I didn't know if I had heard right or if my mind was playing tricks on me. I stopped fucking him and turned back to look at him.

"Who the hell is Angel?" I asked. I had caught an attitude.

"Nobody. Keep going," he said, trying to brush the situation under the rug. He looked embarrassed that he had even said it. I gave him a sideways glare, and then I reluctantly started back up. I decided I needed to face him. I got up off of his dick and turned around and sat back on it.

As I rode him, it felt like everything was going in slow motion. Dragons floated across the room, and the face I saw wasn't the face I usually saw. I kept seeing Omar's text message in my head. I saw my dad lying on the bed with his sunglasses on.

He looked how he did the last time I saw him, over ten years ago. He had that big beer belly, and he didn't say a word. The champagne bottle sat on the bed, and I knew it was now or never. I heard him say it again and again.

That's right, Angel. Fuck Daddy the way ya' Mama couldn't. I picked up the bottle and bashed his face with it. His hands dropped to the bed, and I jumped off of him and went to get my purse. I rummaged through it until I felt the knife that I had wrapped in a napkin. I took the knife out of the napkin, walked over to him, climbed back on top of him, and then I slit his throat from ear to ear. Blood came from his mouth and neck.

Still, I rode him slowly, staring in his eyes. Then I took my two fingers and closed them.

I hopped off of his dick and sat on the bed next to him. I went through one of his pockets and grabbed his wallet. I opened it, and there it was, big as day. His ID. His name was Albert Christopher Jacobs.

My eyes welled up. I felt sick to my stomach. I had just fucked my own father. This was the same man who wanted me dead. I went through the wallet and came across a picture of my little sister, Crystal. I forced a smile. She looked pure and innocent. I flipped it over and it read: ANGEL CRYSTAL JACOBS. AGE EIGHT.

The tears fell slowly. I didn't have a sister. All I had was me.

"There is no Crystal. You are Crystal," I chanted a few times, closing my eyes. I told myself that I was going to face reality. I took a deep breath and one last look at the picture of me. I threw the wallet on the floor and went through his other pocket.

There was his cell phone.

I went through it to see if he was involved with a girl named Porsha. I looked at one of the numbers, which looked all too familiar. I grabbed my phone to compare numbers. I scrolled down to the letter P in my contacts list and clicked VIEW on

Porsha's name. To my surprise, it was the same exact number. I went to view his text messages, and my eyes saw pure hatred. It was clear to me as I read through their back-and-forth texts that both she and Cliff were trying to help my father take me out of the game.

This all just couldn't be true. The world was so small, and it broke my heart that all these people wanted me dead so bad.

I had one down and two to go. I put his phone in my purse and put my purse over my shoulder. I walked to the door, and then I stopped. I set my purse down on the floor and then walked back to where he was lying.

I rubbed his slit throat with my right index finger. I wrote *Closure* on the wall with his blood. I went to the bathroom and washed my hands. The water and blood circled the sink together and then went down the drain. I turned the water off and went to put my clothes back on. I looked at him one last time before spitting in his face. I grabbed my purse from off of the floor, got my keys out of it, and headed out the door He was a sad-ass excuse for a father. *Hate* was a strong word, and since I was a strong woman, it was safe to say I hated him.

Chapter 21

When I woke up, I was in my car across the street from Omar's house. I looked around and saw that it couldn't be any later than seven in the morning. Seeing his car parked let me know that he was inside. I got out of my car and headed to his door. I saw a car pull up. When I looked in its direction, it pulled off.

I watched it as it slowly drove past. After it was out of sight, I knocked on Omar's door. I knocked for almost twenty minutes before he opened the door, rubbing his eyes. I wrapped my arms around him and began kissing him. My heart had led me to his house.

When he was completely awake, he began kissing me back. He laid me on the couch and got on top of me.

He kept whispering, "I love you, Angel."

I said it back, and at that moment, I felt so complete. Finally, I was at ease.

"Promise you won't leave me again?" he said as he looked me dead in the eyes.

"I can't promise," I whispered. I knew he loved me genuinely. His eyes told me so. They weren't bedroom eyes. They were "I'm in love" eyes.

Sirens could be heard distinctively from afar. I knew they were coming for me as I kissed him for the last time.

"Why not?" he asked.

"I'm going to jail, and I may never get out. I came here just to spend my last moment of freedom with you." I started crying, and he wiped my tears away with his hand.

We didn't utter a word as the sirens got closer. Soon we knew they were right outside his door. There were loud, firm knocks, and then a voice shouted, "Omar, your best bet is to open the door!" Omar looked at me, and his expression told me he didn't want to do it.

"Go," I instructed. Either way the dice rolled, I was going to jail. I got up and looked out the window and saw that we were surrounded by cops.

Omar got up and headed to the door. He stopped midway. "Come here," he said and motioned at the same time. I walked over to him, and we embraced. He kissed me on the forehead and then pulled me in and held me tight. "For the first time in my life I'm in love," he said. I knew it hurt him to think that he finally had me back, and now I was leaving him for good.

I slowly opened the door.

They rushed in and grabbed me.

"Angel Jacobs, you are under arrest for the murders of . . ." He so many names to rattle off that I could no longer hear him. I stared at Omar the entire time they cuffed me and read me my rights. When we got off the porch, I saw Kim and Porsha in front of the car I had seen when I first got there. Finally, I knew for sure it was they who had set me up.

I couldn't get mad. All I could do was charge it to the game. Why were they in front of his house, anyway? I couldn't understand why. They put me in the backseat of the police car, and we were on our way to booking.

I was not sure if I was there all the way when I did the things that I did. To be honest, I didn't even remember the majority of the people whose murders they charged me with. I couldn't say if I did or didn't do it, because I couldn't recall it all.

As I lay on the leather chaise in my psychiatrist Dr. Dozey's office, she insisted that I tell her my life story. She told me that she was trying to get me off with the insanity card. I didn't think I was insane, but if it got me out that hellhole, then I was as crazy as I needed to be.

I stared at the ceiling and rubbed my developed stomach. I was five months pregnant by somebody. I wanted it to be Omar's, but after

being hypnotized and Dr. Dozey telling me all
the men I had slept with, there was no telling
who this kid belonged to.

She told me that that was all she needed and
that I was free to go. Too bad it didn't mean I
could literally go free. When I walked out of her
office, there were two sheriffs waiting for me.
My shackled wrists and ankles made noises as I
walked to the police car.

Mr. Bennifeld sat beside me, with his assistant
on the other side of me. Physically, I was in the
courtroom. Mentally, I was somewhere else. This
trial had dragged on for far too long, and today
we would be getting a verdict. Before that, they
decided to finally let my mother testify.

She looked like she would die at any minute.
She looked tired and frail. She sat on the stand,
painting us all a picture. The picture she put
together was one I didn't want to see, let alone
hear.

She recapped the many nights she would
catch my father going in my room, molesting me.
"Ever since, that child ain't been right," she said.
She told them that I was diagnosed with bipolar
disorder around the time I turned fourteen. "She
had become suicidal and tried killing herself.
In the process, she lost a baby," my mother
explained. She knew more than I knew she knew.

They did a DNA test on my unborn baby, and it was proven that my child's dad was indeed my father. I almost threw up. I had made up in my mind that Mike was the father of my baby. I couldn't believe this shit.

My mother told the jury a few incidents that happened to me with my illness. Everyone looked touched and hurt as they listened. After my mother stepped down, Dr. Dozey stood up to take her place.

She swore to tell the truth and nothing less, and then she said, "After doing months and months of studies on Miss Jacobs, it's evident that she was not herself while these things were occurring. In her head, her child's father was keeping her from their daughter. As you heard her mother say, her child never made it to live." She walked up to a board that had a diagram that was supposed to look like my brain.

"Take a look at this side of Angel's brain. As you can see, it's partially shaded. This indicates that she is herself only half of the time. She went around for several years believing in her heart that she was raising her younger sister, but you see, she is the only child. Her younger sister was her when she was younger. She never saw it that way." Dr. Dozey went back to sit down so that the DA could quiz her.

The DA was a handsome young black man. He was clean-cut and had an expensive suit on. I surely wouldn't mind fucking him once or twice. Now wasn't the time to have such thoughts in my head. I couldn't help it, though. He walked up to Dr. Dozey and began to prove his case.

"So, Dr. Dozey, what you are saying is"—he turned to me—"Angel was not mentally there when all of these killings occurred?"

"That is correct."

"So while you were studying her, did you ever figure out why she felt she needed to kill these innocent men?"

"Well, from what I discovered, she saw who she thought was her child's father whenever she slept with someone. She would grow angry, and she would kill them. It was only in her mind that she would finally get to see the child he had kept from her."

The DA smiled and went on to say, "So if we let her off, you mean to tell me every baby mama who sleeps around has the right to kill their alleged baby daddy?" He raised his brow.

"No, I'm not saying that at all," she answered. The jury looked like they were siding with the DA.

"You see, Angel is a mass murderer. There is no other way to put it. She's not crazy in the head. She's just bitter," the DA declared.

At that moment I wanted to spit in his damn face.

He went on. "After she hideously killed her father, she wrote *Closure* with his blood on the wall. If you ask me, she wanted to kill him for all the things he did to her. Now that he's dead, she's at ease. She hasn't killed a soul since then. Like the wall said, she got her closure."

I looked at the jury. Some of them were shaking their head, as if they agreed with him.

"She's a mass murderer. That insanity card is going to let her and a whole lot of other serial killers in this world go kill more people!" He turned to me. "Do you see an insane woman sitting right there?" He turned to the jury and said, "I do not. Before you leave here today, take a look at all these grieving families who lost their loved ones at the hands of this alleged crazy woman." He sat in his chair.

The judge said that we would take a recess while the jury reached a verdict.

I looked behind me and saw my mother and Omar together. The two people I loved the most. Through all the lies, hallucinations, and deaths, they were still here for me, at my side. I didn't know how this would end, but my gut told me it wouldn't end how I had planned for it to.

Mr. Bennifeld was in my ear, telling me that if I was let free, I would have to enroll in counseling.

"You know we took the plea bargain if the judge finds you guilty, right?"

I nodded my head, as if to say yes.

"Okay, just making sure you're clear as to what we have done."

The plea bargain would allow me to serve life in jail, with no death row. I didn't give a damn what we took. Either way it went, I was in jail forever. I looked back at Omar, who mouthed, "I love you." I smiled and mouthed it back.

After three long hours, the jury had come up with a verdict. My heart was in my lap. I had no clue how this was going to surface. Mr. Bennifeld had represented me the best that he could. There was no way that I would be mad at him if I lost the case.

"All rise for Judge Raymond," said the bailiff.

We all stood up as the judge made his way to his seat. "You may now be seated," said the judge once he was back on the bench. We all sat down and awaited my fate. The judge looked over at the jury and asked, "Have you reached a verdict?"

A middle-aged white lady who was standing at a microphone said, "Yes."

"Please read us what you have."

"On this day, October twelve, two thousand nine, we the jury find the defendant, Angel Crystal Jacobs . . ."

To be continued . . .